VULNERABLE VOICES

OWEN B LEWIS

The Book Guild Ltd

First published in Great Britain in 2022 by
The Book Guild Ltd
Unit E2 Airfield Business Park,
Harrison Road, Market Harborough,
Leicestershire. LE16 7UL
Tel: 0116 2792299
www.bookguild.co.uk
Email: info@bookguild.co.uk
Twitter: @bookguild

Copyright © 2022 Owen B Lewis

The right of Owen B Lewis to be identified as the author of this
work has been asserted by them in accordance with the
Copyright, Design and Patents Act 1988.

All rights reserved. No part of this publication may be
reproduced, transmitted, or stored in a retrieval system, in any form or by any means,
without permission in writing from the publisher, nor be otherwise circulated in
any form of binding or cover other than that in which it is published and without
a similar condition being imposed on the subsequent purchaser.

This work is entirely fictitious and bears no resemblance to any persons living or dead.

Typeset in 11pt Minion Pro

Printed and bound in the UK by TJ Books LTD, Padstow, Cornwall

ISBN 978 1915352 163

British Library Cataloguing in Publication Data.
A catalogue record for this book is available from the British Library.

To all the friends I made when I worked in care.
Too many to name but you know who you are.
Thanks for the memories!

PIZZA

Number three, Bower Road. The snow is falling down but not as heavily as it has been. I have to cycle slowly so I won't skid on the icy ground.

Once I reach the house, I ring the doorbell and wait. No one answers for a while. If they don't come to fetch it, I might just open the box and eat the pizza myself. That would at least warm me up.

But just as I'm about to make that thought a reality, the door opens. I recognise her immediately, even though it's been five years. There's no mistaking those glasses. It's Kim. I had no idea she lived here.

'Ellis!' she says in amazement.

I hand over the pizza and don't say anything.

'How are you keeping?' she says. 'It's great to see you. What are you doing these days?'

'Well... this,' I say, pointing to my bike and the pizza boxes. Kim tries to hide her surprise that after all this time, I'm just a pizza boy.

I want to ask Kim if she ever thinks about him. I'm sure she does. But I can't bring myself to ask. Instead, I just ask her about the Hub. Is she still there; is everyone alright?

'Yes, still there,' she says. 'Everyone still talks about you, Ellis. It'd be good if you came to visit, but I'll understand if you don't.'

She smiles sweetly, and I attempt a smile back. She closes the door and I get back on my bike. Heading to my next destination. Number twenty-nine, Archie Street.

There's a man on the kerb. Worn and ripped clothes, and a long shaggy beard that doesn't look like it's been washed for years. He's homeless. I cycle past, then change my mind. I turn around, coming close to him. He looks up, dazed.

'Take this.' I smile.

He looks unsure at first, but I insist. He eventually takes the pizza box from me and opens it.

'Thank you, kind sir,' he says.

'Enjoy,' I say.

Then I cycle on, thinking what story I'll tell. I could just say it fell off, the box opened and the pizza splattered onto the road. Then they'll have to quickly make up a new one for the people at Archie Street.

Yeah, that will do. It's happened to me before. I guess I can't stop caring for the vulnerable, even if I try.

HANDS

The next morning, I sleep in until nearly midday. After a quick shower, I go to pick up Jessica.

Rochelle answers the door and stares at me with hatred. I smile nervously, ask her if she wants me to come inside to help.

'Jessica!' she shouts. 'He's here!'

Her mam turns and trots down the hallway, disappearing into one of the rooms.

From a different archway, Jessica appears, her dad gripping her waist, encouraging her to the door.

'Hello, Ellis,' her father says.

'Hiya, Andy, hiya, Jessica,' I say.

'You take good care of her.' He smiles.

'I always do.'

'That's true. Where are you going today?'

'I thought we'd go for lunch at Nando's.'

'She will like that.'

'I will.' Jessica smiles.

Jessica doesn't usually talk very much, especially with lots of people around. I beam at her, but my eyes are bursting to explode with tears. Every time she speaks I feel like this. She never used to be like that, so when she does find her voice I pray she won't stop, and that wonderful girl would reappear. I miss the days when I wished she would shut up. Now I wish she would talk forever.

'Sorry about Rochelle,' Andy says.

'Please, you don't need to apologise every time. I get it,' I say.

'I know, I just feel bad. You do a lot for our Jessica. I hope you know I don't think any of this is your fault, Ellis. You're a good guy.'

'Thank you,' I say.

I gently put my arm around Jessica as I help her out the door and down the steps. When we get out of the gate and onto the street, I wave goodbye to Andy and walk with Jessica through the snow.

*

I order her favourite meal, chicken nuggets and fries, and a halloumi wrap for myself. As we wait for our food I watch her, and suddenly feel like I'm falling back in time. Our first date was just like this. I remember I was a lot more nervous than she was. That's the only difference to now, really, apart from the fact we are much older and I'm a vegetarian.

Making conversation with Jessica can be quite difficult. I just smile at her, talk about my week, how despite not having been up to much it was a better week than most. I don't mention Kim. I think Jessica only met her once, and she probably wouldn't really remember who she was.

There is a song playing in the background. I couldn't quite hear it at first but then I realised. It's 'Heaven Is a Halfpipe'. I love that song for many reasons.

When our food arrives, I help her pick up her knife and fork. I can feel her arms shake. I guess being a carer never truly leaves you. I never made it into that profession, but it probably isn't that far away from this.

I move my hands away for a second, but she's struggling to cut up her food, so I gently put my hands on top of hers. I look at her and smile. She smiles back, but her eyes look sad. I help her, pressing onto her hands, guiding her but also giving her a sense of independence as she pushes her knife and fork into her food and eventually places it into her mouth of her own accord.

She has her better days. I do see improvements, but days like this would break my heart if it weren't already broken. Before this, she was so independent, so full of potential that it hurts to see her like this. It's not fair at all. I pray that one day she will get fully better, because she had so many hopes and dreams, and I'm scared she will never pursue them. All her confidence has gone, faded. But then, Sonia got a lot better. Could Jessica do the same?

BLOOD

When I get home, I fling the keys on the side and walk into the living room. Zoe's sat on the sofa, watching Orange Is the New Black.

'What you been up to?' she asks.

'Just went out for lunch, then had a walk.'

'I could make something for tea if you like?'

'It's fine,' I say. 'I'll get a takeaway or something after my shift.'

'So, did you just go out on your own then?'

'Yeah,' I say.

I sit down next to her, gazing at the telly but not really taking in what's happening. I fold my arms and let out a sigh.

'What's wrong?' Zoe asks.

'Sorry, I'll go next door.'

'No, it's okay. I'm not really concentrating, just have it on for background noise.'

She has her laptop on her knees. I glance at the screen.

There is a series of very complicated diagrams on it. Zoe is doing a presentation at a big conference next week, and she's always complaining that she's falling behind. I bet she's exaggerating. That girl is always on top of things. And anyway, if she's falling behind, then what does that say about me? Sometimes I wonder if I should even bother to get up.

I head to the kitchen.

'I thought you weren't eating until later?' Zoe calls out.

'Just getting a drink. Something strong.'

'Okay. By the way, are you working tomorrow?'

'Yes.'

'Oh, that's a shame.'

'Why?'

'I was invited to a last-minute get-together, wondered if you wanted to come.'

'I don't socialise.'

'But you should, Ellis. It's not good to keep yourself distant.'

I don't bother to respond. I get the wine out of the cupboard and pour myself a glass.

It's alright for Zoe to socialise. She actually has something interesting to talk about. She's two years younger than me and is a scientist – I'm not entirely sure what kind. Every day she has something to work on and people to talk to.

I swig the drink down in one, then I bang down the glass harder than I was expecting to. The glass shatters and cuts my skin. My hand starts to bleed.

I must have cried out because Zoe runs in to see what's

happened. She quickly gets some kitchen towel and covers it around my hand. Then she collects the glass with a dustpan and brush and chucks them away into the bin.

Then she places her arms around me as I shake in terror. Blood. I hate the sight of it. I always have done, but not to the level I do since that day. That horrible, horrible day.

BENEVOLENT

There was a fire, and after that my life was never the same again.

It happened five years ago, but I remember it like it was yesterday. That's two clichés already, but the ironic thing is that what happened that day was not a cliché at all. Far from it. No one would have expected that the house would have gone up in flames, but it did. Nathan thought I did it, but I said that I didn't. I believed what I said, but after all, Nathan was always right.

Before I knew Nathan, Jessica and I had been dating for two years. We met in sixth form in our chemistry class. It all started when she approached the stool next to me on the first day of sixth form and said, 'You got room for a little one?' Which was strange, because she was actually bigger than me. We'd been at the same school since Year 7, but we didn't know each other back then. I guess we must have been put in different teaching groups at the time and never passed each other in the hallways up until that point.

After our last exam she told me to meet her on the Stray late at night. She didn't say why; it was all very mysterious. Making me wonder preposterous things about why she wanted to meet me there, but as I walked onto the grass, I just assumed there was no special reason. We were in a relationship; of course she wanted to meet up with me. There didn't have to be a reason.

I saw her waiting for me from a distance, standing by a tree. She was wearing her favourite dress – pale purple, like the flowers around her feet. Although it was night, I could tell it was that dress. Her emerald eyes were staring at me and the colour on the dress was reappearing as my eyes adjusted to the dark.

'Hello, Ellis,' she said. She came across as though she had rehearsed what she was about to say, although I couldn't think why. I didn't like to ask. I just smiled and leaned in for a kiss. She stepped away.

'Is everything alright?' I asked.

'Can we walk?'

'Sure.'

We walked further along the Stray and down into town. She didn't say much, which was unusual because she normally talked nineteen to the dozen. We walked past shops and trees, then down a slope that led us past more shops and a hotel. We ended up in Valley Gardens, where we passed more trees and flowers. She stopped walking when we stepped onto the stone floor of the Sun Pavilion. This was the place we went on our first date, after our meal at Nando's.

Jessica got down on one knee and I thought, *Is she*

really going to do what I think she is going to do? She was always in favour of girls doing things like that. I looked down and it turned out she was just tying up her Converse shoes. She got up, and again, she just looked at me.

'Thought you were going to propose to me then for a second,' I said, half-jokily.

'Ellis, I am moving to Bath.' Her face was inexpressive when she said this.

'Bath? What, why?'

'Because I got accepted there to do a BA in Contemporary Circus.'

'Contemporary Circus?'

'Yes, it's like a sort of theatre course.'

'But I thought we agreed we weren't going to do further education.'

'I know, but this course came up, and it looked a lot of fun.'

'Right, well, that's great. I guess I will have to start looking for jobs in Bath then.'

'There's no need.'

'Why?'

'Because, well… Ellis, you don't need to come with me.'

'But I am your boyfriend.'

She sighed. 'I'm breaking up with you.'

'But why?'

She looked at the ground and then across to the other side of the garden towards a late-night jogger with a little dog chasing behind. She then looked straight back at me, an expression like she was juggling thoughts instead of balls.

'What is it? Jessica, have I done something wrong?'

Her body suddenly stood still and her eyes were full of repentance. She seemed herself at last. 'You haven't done anything wrong.'

'Then what is it you're trying to say?'

'Ellis, what we had… it was fun. I enjoyed it, but we are getting older. It won't be long till we're both eighteen and we've got our whole lives ahead of us.'

'Yes, and…'

She sighed with irritation and started to walk around in circles.

'Jessica, please just tell me what the problem is.'

She stopped wandering around. 'Ellis, I want a fresh start. I will be going to university after this summer, and I want everything to be brand new. New city, new flat, new friends and new—'

'Boyfriend,' I said, finishing her sentence for her.

Her eyes became repentant again. She didn't say anything.

'I thought we were in love,' I said.

'No, it wasn't love, Ellis.'

'Then what was it?'

'It was a relationship, but it wasn't love. Love is found later in life, after you explore the world and get to understand yourself.'

'Right,' I said. I didn't know what else to say at the time. I loved Jessica, and I'd thought she loved me. How did I miss that?

'So you're breaking up with me?'

'I'm sorry,' she said.

'But I thought we were perfect for each other.'

'No. We have some similarities and interests, but that isn't love, Ellis.'

'Then what is love?'

'You know it when it hits you.'

But I did know. Why was she talking to me as if she understood my feelings better than I did?

'Ellis,' she said. She placed her hand on my cheek. 'You're a kind-hearted person. In fact, in Welsh your name means "benevolent".' (Where was she going with this?) 'You will find someone who will fall in love with you, but it isn't me. I have short hair and flat breasts and I like JLS. That's the wrong reasons to love a girl, Ellis. You got to find someone to fall in love with for the right reasons.'

I remember at the time I thought, *What on Earth is this girl on about?* but I think now I understand what she meant. But how she could have known, I don't think I will ever be able to work out.

'Goodbye, Ellis. Thanks. You were good to me.' She then kissed me on my cheek and walked away.

I watched her, with my hand on my face and my mouth opened wide as she walked away. Her body dissolving into the air.

PHOENIX

I cried all night whilst listening to JLS on repeat. The next day, I woke up at 7:30 in the morning. I thumped my clock to stop the alarm. I must have forgotten to change the settings, as I didn't need to wake up this early anymore. I had no school, no job to go to, no girlfriend to entertain. I still couldn't believe how she'd acted last night. She was so theatrical. Maybe she was already trying to get into that mindset so she could find it easy to settle in on her new course.

I lay in my bed wide awake. My whole body was underneath my duvet covers, except for my arms, which were folded on top. I was staring up crossly at the cracks in the ceiling.

I was disturbed by the sound of a creak next to my door. I looked over and saw my mam peering through. 'Planning to get up?'

'What's the point?' I said.

'What do you mean?'

'I got no school, and I got no job to get to.'

'Well, perhaps you should look for a job.'

'But it's not that easy, is it? You can't just get a job even if you look for one. Not these days.'

'Well, you've got to try.'

Her floating head disappeared. I sighed and looked back at the ceiling. After a while, the smell of English breakfast was wafting through my door. Bacon, sausage, beans, mushrooms, egg and toast. Mam knew how to get me up.

I jumped out of bed quickly and pulled my dressing gown around me. I hurried to the bathroom and gave myself a quick soak. Once I got out, I headed back into my bedroom and put on some clothes. Then I ran down the stairs and into the kitchen.

Mam was keeping watch over the cooker and Dad was hidden inside his newspaper. When I sat down, he lowered the newspaper and looked directly at me. 'You were out late last night. Celebrating the last day at school?'

'I wish.'

'Then what were you doing?' he asked, folding his newspaper in half.

'I was with Jessica.'

'I see.'

Mam came over with two plates in her hand. She put one each in front of me and Dad. The smell of the food rose up into our nostrils like the ashes from a phoenix. I needed this comfort, as Jessica had taken it all away from me the previous night.

Dad and I started eating our food as Mam sat down

close to us with her own plate. She took a bite of her toast, chewed it and then gulped it down with a sip of tea.

'So,' she said, 'it looks like we need to get you a job.'

'Do I have to?' I said.

'Well, it's either that or looking into a course at university, but you told me that you and Jessica didn't want that.'

'Well, I might want to now.'

'What made you change your mind?' said Mam.

'She did,' I said.

'What do you mean?'

'Jessica, she's moving to Bath to do a course in Contemporary Circus.'

'What kind of clown degree is that?' Dad said. He looked to me and then Mam to see if either of us found his pun funny, but neither of us did.

'Oh,' said Mam. 'So, how will you and Jessica keep in touch? Are you thinking of moving with her? If so, you really will need to start washing your own pants.'

'Jessica has broken up with me.'

Mam and Dad stopped eating and looked at each other, and then looked right at me.

'I'm sorry, Ellis,' said Mam.

'It's fine,' I said.

They both looked at me as if they knew it wasn't. Why did everyone treat me like they knew how I felt more than I did? 'I'm fine, honestly,' I said.

I looked down at my plate and continued eating.

'Let's not worry about what you're going to do until after your birthday,' said Mam brightly.

'Good idea,' I said as I took a spoonful of beans and put them into my mouth.

'Is there anything you would like to do on your birthday? Anything special?'

'Not really.'

'But it's your eighteenth.'

I looked up at her. 'Can I think about it and get back to you?' I said.

'Of course. Sorry, Ellis. I am sure Jessica will realise she has made a mistake.'

'Leave it, Sandra, the boy can sort this out for himself,' said Dad. 'We shouldn't meddle in such things.'

'You're right, Barry,' she said. 'Things will work out for Ellis, let's not get too down about it.'

'I will do my best,' I said, but I don't think they realised I was still there.

'And don't worry about what he's going to do next,' said Mam, ignoring me. 'He's got the whole summer to sort that out.'

'If it's a job he wants, he's going to have a hard time finding one. His CV only has "paperboy" written on it,' said Dad. 'And he lied about that.'

'Well, he's got to start somewhere,' Mam said.

'The Tories are back in charge – well, the ones that aren't hiding behind red ties. They are making it harder for working-class boys like Ellis to start a career.'

'Well, perhaps he could volunteer during the summer, find something to occupy himself while he decides what to do,' said Mam. 'Gain some skills, and then you never know… he could get picked up by the company and get paid.'

'Volunteer?' said Dad. 'Give over, that's exactly what the Tories want you to do. What's this country coming to?' He shook his head.

'You wouldn't want to volunteer at mine or your dad's workplace?' Mam asked me.

So I hadn't turned invisible then…

I shook my head.

'To be independent he needs to find a job where he hasn't got us by his side,' said Dad. 'You can't mother Ellis forever, Sandra.'

'That wasn't what I was saying, Barry,' she said.

'Besides, he couldn't work with you. He fainted when he cut his knee two years ago.'

'He didn't faint from the cut; he fainted from the heat. It was a very hot day and he didn't drink any water. I remember it well.'

'Well, he hates hospitals, and he also hates the smell of oil, so he couldn't work at the garage with me either.'

'Can I be excused?' I said.

Neither of them answered. They just continued bickering at one another, so I got out of my chair and headed back to my room. I lay on my bed reading *Under Milk Wood* by Dylan Thomas. This made me think of Jessica when she told me that my name meant 'benevolent' in Welsh. She said that it fitted who I was. If that was true, then why did she leave me? As I thought of her I wept into the pages of my book.

CLOCK

All I did for the next two weeks was listen to music and masturbate. On July 21st, the day before my birthday, I lay on my bed and thought about how the day was going extremely slowly. It was one o'clock in the afternoon and both my parents were at work. Nearly every day since Jessica dumped me, time had felt slow. Maybe when I fiddled with the settings of my alarm clock I changed the speed of the universe.

I thought about giving Jessica a ring, and then decided it was better if I didn't, so I rang Joel instead. 'Why haven't you been in touch?' were my first words to him.

'Hello to you too,' he replied.

'Well, why haven't you?'

'Sorry, I been busy helping my brother move out.'

'You free now?'

'Sure.'

'Great, meet me at mine and then we can head into town.'

SURPRISE

Joel and I got a takeaway pizza and sat with it on the bench opposite the Queen Victoria Monument. Joel was pushing back his hair as he helped himself. He was younger than me but a lot taller.

'Jessica broke up with me,' I told him.

'Ah, man, that sucks,' he said.

I was hoping he was going to say something with a bit more wisdom than that. But that was Joel. He never went into deep conversations unless it was about tennis or racing car driving. (Why were we even friends?)

'I lost my virginity to her because I thought she was the one.'

'That's rough,' he said.

I sighed as I watched a crisp packet fly across the kerb. 'It's my birthday tomorrow,' I said.

'I know, your mam invited me.'

I looked at him as if he had just told me he worked for MI5. 'What do you mean, invited you? Invited you to what?' I said.

SURPRISE

'Your surprise birthday party.'

'She never told me about this.'

'That's because it's a surprise.'

'Great,' I said.

Two minutes later Joel slapped himself on the forehead. 'Don't tell your mam I ruined the surprise, will you?'

'Don't worry. I won't.'

After we ate our pizza, we wandered around the town, hanging out in Game and walking the streets. Then, Joel drew my attention to something up ahead. A girl with short dark hair was walking towards me. It was Jessica. She was with Melissa and Sian.

'Oh, hey, Ellis,' she said.

'Not in Bath yet then?' I said.

'No, I am just heading to the shops to buy some things for my new flat.'

'Great,' I said. 'Well, me and Joel, we're just hanging out.'

'Cool,' she said.

We stared at each other for a while.

'I hope there's nothing bad between us?' she said as she bit her lip.

'No, not at all,' I said sarcastically.

'Great, well, I'll see you at the party.' She smiled.

'What party?' I said.

'Your party.'

'Great,' I said.

FUTURE

After I left Joel to wander back to his, I headed home. My mam and dad were watching *The Chase*. I sat down close to them.

'What you been up to?' asked Dad.

'Not much. I just went around the town centre with Joel.'

'You're still friends with that kid?'

'Yes.' Though I wasn't sure why. We didn't have anything in common anymore. I didn't know why Jessica thought I was kind-hearted. If I was kind-hearted then I would have more friends and I wouldn't think bad thoughts about the one friend I did have.

'If you go out at all tomorrow, make sure you're back at six o'clock,' said Mam.

'Okay,' I said.

Then I saw her look at my dad. He gave her a wink and they both smiled. They were in on a secret.

I couldn't believe it. It was kind of them to go out

FUTURE

of their way to make me a surprise birthday party, but I wasn't sure I was up for it. I wasn't feeling in the mood. Tomorrow I would officially be an adult, and I would have to have responsibilities. I'd thought I was going to be alright because Jessica was in the same boat as me. But not now. She had 'plans' and a future set up for herself. She'd pushed me out of the boat and now I was drowning in the sea.

I hoped I'd get a job soon. Volunteer or a paid job, I didn't care. I just wanted something that would distract me from Jessica. I did Chemistry, Drama, ICT and English in sixth form, but I didn't think I wanted to go down any of those paths. After tomorrow I was going to have to think of my future, and I didn't think I was ready.

TOILET

In the morning I got up earlier than I had the previous day, but my parents were already up. Mam was reading the *TV Choice* and sipping her tea. Dad was watching the telly, but they both stopped what they were doing as soon as I came in.

'Happy birthday to you,' they sang. I thanked them and sat on the chair opposite the sofa. Without a word, Dad nodded at the gift bag of presents on the coffee table.

I opened them up. I'd been given a guide to life (and it wasn't even the Bart Simpson one) and a driving test theory book. I guess when you reach eighteen, the fun presents are a thing of the past. I remember when my presents used to be Pokémon games, guides to life (the Bart Simpson one) and *Friends* DVDs. Though, thinking about it, couldn't they have got me the driving test theory book last year?

'Thank you very much,' I said. I tried to sound pleased, but I'm a rubbish actor.

'That's not everything,' said Dad. 'The wrapping paper is a present in itself.'

TOILET

I picked up the bits of old newspaper that I'd ripped off. They'd been cut from the local paper and listed the companies that were hiring in the area. Terrific.

Isn't it strange how we are always working towards the future? The future doesn't exist, because whenever it does it becomes the present. Like all the gifts I was given that day. They were things for the future that became present, or presents in this case.

Before Mam and Dad left me to go to work, they reminded me to be back before six if I was planning on going out. Then they stared at me as if they were expecting me to ask the reason why. But I just nodded and went to my room. I knew what they had planned. I was dreading it. My cousins Ryan and Jenny had both left Harrogate and I was sure Aunty Mel wasn't coming, so it was going to be the most depressing party of all time: my ex-girlfriend, my friend who isn't really a friend, my parents, oh, and Nana. I was sure they were going to bring Nana. Don't get me wrong, I love my nana to bits. My parents must have found it odd that I hadn't asked why Nana hadn't rung or sent me any gifts. I felt bad about that. But I'd make up for it when they brought her round later.

I rested on my bed, turning the pages of the books I'd been given. The driving theory looked difficult. It came with a DVD where you could take mock theory tests. I placed it into my laptop and gave it a go. I failed. No surprise, really, I guess I had to get revising. But not today; today was my birthday. I looked at the guide to life and started giving that a read.

Introduction – So you're now in the real world, time to start dreaming...

Life is something you're born into without any thoughts of your own. When you reach adulthood, I am afraid thinking is required.

Don't believe the crap they tell you in other books! This book is the truth. So, don't live in the present because the present doesn't last long, but the future does.

This book will guide you in the right direction. It will help you succeed in all your desires. The ones you know about and the ones you don't even realise you have.

Read on and you will find out what to work towards. This book tackles soulmates, sex, a career, a roof over your head. How to get the perfect CV, how to get the right grades, how to find the right job. You will also learn how to deal with the different types of people that you will face in the world. The real world. It's shit, so think of us as your pooper scooper. We will clear the shit away, and bring you to paradise. Because paradise can be found when shit disappears. Life is like a toilet. If you can flush, then you can get by. Life is shit, but yours doesn't have to be. Find the good underneath the bad.

Where the heck did they find this? I thought. The book said some weird shit, literally.

BALLOONS

Surprisingly, the day went quicker than the last couple of weeks. I spent the whole day listening to the One Direction album. It was brilliant. I even danced around in just my underpants as I mimed the songs I knew best and played air guitar to the ones I didn't. I even spotted the neighbour through the window. I wasn't sure if she was shocked or just enjoying the show. For a laugh, I pulled my pants off and swung them around my fingers.

I guess it's odd to like boy bands at eighteen, especially if you're a guy. But I've never understood why. After all, One Direction were guys of about my age. I wished I was like them, singing songs for a living, doing photoshoots and having thousands of girls screaming at me. I'd have liked to have been a pop star; that would be an easy life. Especially if you were pampered like this lot.

I'd have liked a birthday present like this album: something that didn't pressure me about my future, but a CD with songs about falling in love, or being in love, or wanting love. Then I remembered that Jessica seemed to think I didn't know anything about love, so at the end of the day, even my favourite CD just became another educational object to help me onto the next step.

Eventually I heard someone come through the door. I ran out of my bedroom to see who it was. It was Mam, with bags full of shopping. It must have been five-thirty already.

'Hi, Ellis,' she said as she looked up at the top of the stairs. 'Your dad is coming around soon; he's bringing a surprise guest.'

'Okay, is it Nana?' I said.

She nodded. 'But sound surprised when you see her.'

'I will.'

'I just remembered when I parked up that I forgot to get tuna, and it's all your nana eats these days. I don't want her feeling left out when I lay out the par... sorry, forget that last bit,' she said.

'It's fine, Mam. I know about the surprise party. Thanks.'

'Okay, well, still try and look surprised when the time comes. I still need tuna, so if you could go and get some and try to get back as quickly as you can, that would be great.'

'Okay, I will.'

'But get changed first. I know it's your birthday, but a birthday suit isn't really an option.'

Mam then looked down at the floor and hurried through the hallway and into the kitchen, as she heaved the heavy bags along with her. My whole body went red.

BALLOONS

I'd forgotten I'd spent most of the afternoon wearing nothing.

I ran to my room, got dressed and made it out of the house. I walked to the nearest supermarket, which was a fifteen-minute walk. For the whole journey there and back, I thought about Jessica. About how it was only a year ago we went to an outdoor festival together, and it rained, and we didn't care. We just sang and sang, to Katy Perry, Olly Murs and Black-Eyed Peas. And we kissed and drank beer. In between the pop acts we talked, and I would watch her because the beauty of what she was saying would show on her beautiful face. When we made it back to our tent, we had sex and it was wonderful. I held her close and recited sweet poetry, which I then admitted was actually lyrics from a Dizzee Rascal song, so she laughed, and then I laughed. The knickers and bra that she threw into the corner of the tent got damp from the rain that had somehow got through, even though the guy at the shop had insisted the tent was waterproof. But that didn't matter. As long as we were together.

Now she had dumped me, and for some reason she thought it was okay to still come to my birthday party. I guess she still liked me, but she didn't love me after all. I was a fool not to have realised this before she told me.

As I made it back onto my street, I realised I was ten minutes late, but I didn't think that was a problem. I saw balloons waving outside my parents' house, so they must have been ready and waiting for me. I stared at the balloons. Red, yellow, blue and green. They were meant to be the epitome of fun. But in fact, they were just a prison for trapped air, and if they popped they would make a noise like a bomb. Bombs were certainly not the epitome of fun.

Inside the lights would all be off, and I would do the clichéd thing that people do on television shows when they are about to be thrown a surprise birthday party, which is shout out, 'Is anybody there?' Then I would walk into the kitchen, lights would be turned on and everyone would shout, '*Surprise!*' into my face. The sad thing is there would only be five people there, whereas on TV they would have about fifty.

I thought, *What if I just run? What would happen then?* I couldn't do that, though. I loved my mam and dad too much. They did at least try to do things to keep me happy. Which is why, on days like this, I got a sense of guilt.

I let out a sigh and then walked inside.

As suspected, the lights were out. I thought I might as well go along with the whole charade.

'Mam? Dad? What's going on? Is anybody there?' I said, playing along. 'Is there a power cut?' I added. I don't think they say that on the telly. There we are, something different for a change.

As soon as I made it into the kitchen, the lights went on and everyone in the kitchen shouted at me: '*Surprise!*'

Mam, Dad, Nana, Joel, Jessica and Christopher. *What's Christopher doing here?* I thought at the time. *And why does he have his arm around Jessica?*

I looked at him with hatred, and then I looked at Jessica with anger, and then I looked at Mam, who was smiling nervously. I think she was surprised that Jessica had turned up with another boy as well.

'Happy birthday to my favourite grandson,' said Nana as she stumbled over to me.

'I am your only grandson,' I said.

'Yes, that's why. Come on, give us a kiss.'

I bent down, as Nana was half my size. She gave me a kiss on the cheek and then handed me a present.

'Thanks, Nana,' I said. 'Shall I open it now?'

'Yes, go on,' she said.

I unwrapped it, while all the faces in the room were staring at me. Inside was a book by Stephen King. 'I hope you like it,' said Nana.

I said I was sure I would. Then there was an awkward silence until Mam shouted, 'Who wants cake?'

Dad turned the CD player on and JLS started playing. Mam went to slice the cake and Nana sat down after I gave her a big 'thank-you' hug. Joel grabbed a slice of cake before even coming over to wish me a happy birthday. Jessica, though, came straight over to chat to me, although I wished she hadn't.

'Happy birthday, Ellis,' she said.

'Thanks,' I said sarcastically.

'Yeah, happy birthday, mate,' said Christopher, after eventually acknowledging me. (Mate. Did he seriously call me mate? He bullied me for three years in school once he found out I was into painting my nails. I mean, women do it, why can't men?) 'Jessica is a great girl,' he added.

Well, I already knew that.

Joel eventually came over and handed me his present.

His face was covered with buttercream. I opened it, and inside were two copies of *Nuts* magazine. 'Are they still making these?' I asked.

'I'm not sure,' he said. 'These are old copies.'

That explained why the pages were stuck together.

Jessica's nose went up in the air, and her mouth opened. Her eyebrows crossed. It was if someone had stuck a pair of smelly socks in front of her.

'Thanks,' I said to Joel. 'It's the thought that counts.'

I went out of the room, ran upstairs and threw the magazines into the bin. I then went into the bathroom and washed my hands vigorously with soap. When I came back down I saw Christopher heading out the front door.

'Oh, you're leaving already?' I said in hope.

'Nah, mate, just popping out for a cigarette.'

When I made it into the kitchen, Jessica was talking to Nana, and Mam and Dad were chatting with Joel.

When she saw me, Jessica moved away from Nana and stood close to me. 'Ellis, me and Chris will be making a move shortly, but before we do can I have a quick word in private?'

'Sure,' I said.

We went up to my bedroom.

'Your nana's lovely,' she said.

'I know,' I said, as I sat side by side with her on my bed.

'In fact, your whole family is lovely.'

'Thanks.'

'I hope you're not mad at me about the other night.'

'I'm not mad,' I lied. 'What would I be mad about?'

'Because I just dumped you there on the spot, out of the blue, no warning.'

'Right.'

'Well, I hope you know that I do like you very much. But it was never going to work out.'

'I guess not,' I said.

There was an awkward pause until I eventually said, 'So if you split up with me so you can start your new adventure in Bath, why were you already seeing another guy?'

She looked blankly at me. 'What do you mean?' she said. At the time I thought she was having me on, but looking back, somehow, I think she was genuinely puzzled by what I had accused her of.

'Christopher!' I said.

'Oh, no, we're just friends. Don't be silly, Ellis. Please don't assume that I left you for him and that I made the whole Bath thing up so I could leave you.'

'I wasn't saying that.'

'That's good,' she said.

'But why was he all over you and acting like your boyfriend then?'

'I don't know. It's not my fault boys get the wrong impression of me.'

'Don't you think you perhaps lead boys on?'

'I am going to forget you said that, Ellis,' she snapped. 'I know you're better than that. I know you better than you know yourself.'

'How?'

'I just do,' she said.

She then got up and walked towards my CD player. She picked up the One Direction CD that was resting close to it and nodded her approval.

'Everyone fancies the curly-haired one, don't they?' I nodded. 'I like the Irish one – he reminds me of you.'

'I like Louis,' I said.

'Why?' she asked.

'Best voice.'

'Best eyes as well.'

She looked back at my CDs. Her eyes travelled to *Battleground* by The Wanted. 'Oh, brilliant, I love this album. I've got it too.'

'You do?'

'Yeah. Got it on the day it came out.'

'Then why did we not play it when we were together?'

'I don't know.'

'Right.'

She opened up her bag, which she had hanging from her shoulder, and handed me a present.

'Thanks,' I said. 'You didn't have to.'

'I did,' she said.

I opened it up and it was a frame with a picture of the two of us inside. We both had grins so big that they were almost falling out of our cheeks and off our faces.

The picture was taken on our first anniversary. I felt a weird feeling inside my body. The feeling resembled walking into an electric fence. I looked up from the picture of Jessica with her smile up to the Jessica who was standing right by me, still with a smile, but it was a different smile to the one in the picture. This one was less sincere.

BALLOONS

'I love you,' I said.

'No, you don't,' she said.

When I made it back into the kitchen with Jessica, Christopher was back and he was showing off the tattoos all over his arms to my nana. Then Jessica said goodbye to everyone, and I led her and Christopher out of the front door.

Christopher left first and headed to his car. So he could drive already, impressive. Jessica turned to me. 'Have a good life, Ellis. I am sure we will see each other again.'

'I could visit you in Bath?'

'Bath? Oh, yes, maybe,' she said. 'Goodbye, Ellis.' She kissed me on the cheek. I waved to her as she went down the steps and out through my gate.

I watched her get in the car and drive away with Christopher. Then I closed the door and went back to the kitchen for the fourth time that evening.

The cake was all gone. I didn't even get a chance to have a slice.

Joel came and chatted for a bit and then he said he had to leave as he was meeting a girl. 'Congratulations,' I said.

'Thank you,' he said, missing the sarcasm.

While Dad and Mam were tidying and washing up, I picked at what was left of the buffet as I chatted to Nana. 'You look just like your father did when he was your age,' Nana said.

'Really?' I said.

'Really.'

She asked me how I'd done with my exams, and I told her that I passed them all. Two Bs, a C and one A.

'That's very good, Ellis, but you're not planning on doing any courses? Jessica was telling me she was going to be studying in Bath.'

I told her that I had no idea what I wanted to do. The truth was that I wanted to be a singer, but if I told anyone that they would laugh at me (well, maybe not Nana). Singers are meant to be able to sing, look good and be charismatic. I was none of those things. Nana would disagree, which is exactly why I didn't tell her. If I punched a dog, she would still love me. (Just want to make it clear that this was an example of how much my nana loved me. I would never actually punch a dog. Dogs are the most beautiful and kind-hearted creatures out there. We used to have one called Foxy, as she looked more like a fox than a dog. The whole family loved her, and the day she died was a very dark time for us all. So, yeah, I would never do such a thing; neither should anyone else. Dogs are benevolent.)

Anyway, I told Nana that I didn't know what I wanted to do, but maybe it was best to get a job and possibly do a course at university later in life? 'Well,' she said, 'there are always jobs being advertised on the noticeboard of Gina's hair salon. Most of them these days are voluntary, but I assume you're probably looking for paid work, aren't you?'

'Anything will do for now, anything to gain experience.'

'Well, I'm going to Gina's tomorrow,' she said. 'If I see anything I'll pass it on to your father and he can inform you.'

BALLOONS

'Great, thanks, Nana,' I said.

'No problem.' She smiled.

After Mam and Dad had cleared the leftover food and taken down the party balloons and banners, Dad drove Nana back to her house. When he got back, me and my parents watched a movie. Then I started the book that Nana gave me. Finally, a present that wasn't meant for future-planning. Then I thanked my parents for the effort they went through to give me a nice birthday.

When I was ready for bed, I went up to my room and took out the magazines that Joel got me. I pleasured myself and then threw them quickly back into the bin and washed my hands. Then I put my One Direction CD on and listened to it as I tried to sleep.

The last things I remember before nodding off were Louis and then Aston from JLS. They were my favourites; their voices were the best…

GIG

After the fire, I stopped listening to One Direction. I stopped listening to music pretty much altogether. The only time I bothered was when I went to a gig with Jessica a few years ago. Her dad got us tickets to see McBusted. I tried to pull out, but he insisted I came along. So I did. On the car journey he talked about the times Jessica and I used to listen to our music. He said he'd never got One Direction, but McFly and Busted were alright. I was in the back, wondering what Jessica was thinking. She sat by her father in the front passenger seat.

Once we got to the venue and found our seats in the balcony area, I looked around at all the heads that made up the crowd. When I sat down I felt something stick to my jeans. I tried wiping it off, but then got distracted when the lights dimmed and the crowd gave out a massive roar of excitement.

When the band came on, the whole atmosphere became even more loud and energetic. I turned to look at Jessica. I thought watching her enjoy herself might help me. It didn't. She had a smile on her face, but I could tell she was lost and empty inside. Music usually helps people when they're going through difficult times, but for me and Jessica, it seemed silence would have brought more comfort.

Nathan wouldn't have liked me being there. But at the same time, I am sure he would have wanted me to be happy. But was I happy? Not really.

Jessica didn't say one word all night. I thought about the time her dad took us to One Direction's first tour. She sang along to all their songs and told Andy trivia about them that he probably wasn't even taking in. How times change.

WANTED

Nana got back to me with two jobs. One at a different garage to the one Dad was working for, so no chance I was taking that. I hated the smell of oil. Then there was one at a chip shop, which I didn't fancy either. I hated the smell of oil. Mam said I shouldn't be picky, so in the end I did apply for the chip shop job, but luckily they didn't take me on.

I did look in my new Guide to Life to see if it said anything helpful about applying for jobs.

> When looking for a job there are a few things to think about before you apply.
>
> 1. Is it the right job for me?
>   Do I have the right skills and qualifications that they are asking for?
> 2. Is it something that could lead me to other opportunities?

WANTED

If the answer is yes to all the questions listed above, there's a good chance that you're lying (which is a good thing to do to get you by in the real world), or that you're too qualified for your own good.

Just kidding! Congratulations! You should apply!

But of course, life is never that straightforward. You could be the perfect person for the job and they still may not take you on.

Starting out in the world of employment means that you are likely to not have a lot on your CV, and yet that's what they say they are looking for. They want you to be experienced and you may not be. It's a catch-22 – not the book, but the metaphor.

How to make your CV look awesome:

- Lie about everything
- Use big font so it looks like you have more to say than you probably do

Tell them you have good skills in –

- Teamwork
- Communication
- Listening
- Dealing with customers
- Time-keeping
- Organising

They love that bollocks!

> Having said all that, the harsh reality of the real world is that a lot of the time people get employed because they are a family member of someone already working there, or a friend, or they slept with the boss, or they have worked in similar territory with their company before. You're told to build yourself up, and yet that doesn't seem to matter.
>
> Don't let this reality upset you. Remember, life is shit, so as long as you have a pooper scooper at the ready, you can swing the shit out of the way and clear your path by spreading disinfectant everywhere. Make your future smell sweet.

I sent my CV out to music shops as well, as that was the only thing I was interested in at the time. Music, it's the only thing you can do where you can switch your brain off and allow other people's thoughts in that are not your own. I miss being able to do that. These days I am always thinking negative thoughts.

Anyway, none of the music shops took me on. All of them sent me rejection emails and never even gave me any information on why I wasn't successful. I was about to give in, but one day when I was in the middle of town, I walked past this building which I had never noticed before, which was strange because it was at the end of a street I always passed. The building itself was just plain white and attached to many other buildings that all looked the same. I think the reason I took it in that time was because there was a large poster hanging by the gate. It said,

'VOLUNTEERS WANTED'.

Well, I would have preferred to be paid, but at least it was a job. This could be a great way to gain skills and I thought they might even take me on properly in the future. That's what Mam had said when she'd talked about volunteering.

I went through the gate and up to the door. The inside was the complete opposite to the outside. The walls were maroon and the lamps that hung from the walls gave off a tranquil atmosphere. As soon as I got inside, I was greeted by a man with a young-looking face but hair receding from his head.

'Hello!' he said.

'Hi. What is this place?'

'It's a printing office!' he said brightly.

'Ben, it's lunchtime,' said a woman's voice.

Then Lottie appeared. I think she was in her mid-sixties, with light shoulder-length hair and half-moon glasses. She looked at me and smiled. 'Hello, love, is there anything I can help you with?' Her voice was warm and cosy, like the inside of the building.

'I saw you're advertising for volunteers and wondered if I could get more information?' I asked.

Ben smiled and reached out his hand. 'Welcome aboard,' he said. (Was it really that easy to join?)

I laughed and shook his hand. 'Thank you.'

'I'm Ben, and this is Lottie.'

'Hi, I'm Ellis.'

Lottie knocked on the door to my right. She peered in

and said, 'Kim, there's a young man wanting information on how he can volunteer for us.'

The door swung open and a woman who at the time I thought was in her late thirties greeted me, although I'm sure now that she was at least fifty. She was dressed in a professional blouse and skirt, but her green wing-shaped glasses showed her real personality. A woman who still went out to drink on a Friday night and sang at the karaoke bars. But here in the office, she kept that on the downlow. She had a massive smile, like the keys of a piano across her face. She was nice and all, but she was in the wrong job. That woman was meant to be on the stage.

She gave me some forms to read, which would tell me about what they did, their policies and what they'd expect of me. I thanked her and told her that I would get them back to her. She joked that I might change my mind after reading all the paperwork, but I said that I was sure I wouldn't.

Then Ben interrupted and said that he was going to be my boss and that he was Kim's boss as well. Kim laughed nervously. 'Now, Ben, remember what I said before. We are a team.'

'No, I am the boss, and I will tell Ellis what he needs to do.'

'Come on, matey,' said Lottie. 'If you don't eat your lunch, I'll have to eat it for you,' and then she ran all the way down the hall like a little girl, making munching noises.

Ben laughed at this, then looked at me and Kim. 'What's she like?' he said, shaking his head in disbelief.

Then he chased after her. Kim shook her head and smiled at me.

'What's he like, more like,' grunted a voice from behind the door.

I peered over Kim's shoulder and saw a woman typing away on her computer. She was sat over her desk, her back curved.

Kim shut the door and smiled nervously. 'Well, thanks for considering us. Sorry, what did you say your name was?'

'Ellis,' I said.

'Ellis, that's a lovely name. I'm Kim.'

She held out her hand and I shook it, then I noticed that my eyes were staring where they shouldn't be. I went red, said thank you and that I'd be in touch, and then I hurried out the door.

INK

When I got home, I showed my parents the forms. I told them that I had to read through and fill them in, and then I would get a meeting with the boss, which was definitely Kim and not Ben. I did like Ben, though, nice fellow. Kim and Lottie were lovely too. But I wasn't sure about the other woman, who I found out later was called Irene.

'What happens when you meet the boss again?' Dad asked.

'I just do an induction, and then I presume I start.'

'Great, well, get to it,' he said.

I did. I went to my room and read through everything. I found out that the place I was applying for wasn't just a printing office but an office that supported adults with mental illnesses and learning disabilities. As I got to know him later, I came to realise that Ben had Down's Syndrome.

Over tea my dad said, 'A printing job?'

I told him that they made booklets, flyers, posters,

business cards... That sort of thing for walk-in or over-the-phone customers.

'And you say you hate oil, but you can cope with ink?'

'Ink is fine,' I said.

'So is oil, but that doesn't stop you.'

THERAPY

I can smell sausages. Zoe must be making herself some lunch. I'm sat in the living room, but the sound of the gas and the sizzling of the oil in the pan is making my skin crawl. My fingers dig tightly into my legs. I can't cope, even with the telly on loud.

I get up and go outside.

I can't cook food anymore; I have to eat in pubs or restaurants, or I have some of what Zoe's having, when she's not cooking meat. But sometimes I can't even cope with that. I thought that over time I would improve, but instead it seems I am getting worse.

There's too much danger that can be had in a kitchen. Too much. Thank God I don't work in the kitchens at the pizzeria. If I had to I would leave. It would bring back too much trauma from my past. I just collect and deliver, and that's enough for me.

I walk around our neighbourhood and breathe the air. Along the Stray, I pass crocus blossoms which are now visible

THERAPY

as the snow finally begins to melt. The radiant sun glistens on the remaining snow and turns the grass luminous green. The trees look bare, waiting for spring to rise so they can fill their branches with the warmth and soul of their leaves. I can feel new life itching to be born and hear birds up above singing their harmonious melodies.

I end up in town and I pass a block where I once went for help. I went there for therapy, but that didn't seem to work. All I did was tell them what was wrong, and they would just nod like those wobble heads you find at the front of some people's cars. They had no cure, because when you become mentally unstable, there isn't one. Just coping mechanisms, and the only one that worked for me I already knew about, which was going for long walks. I've always enjoyed walking. Somehow it helps my mind go blank, and I don't have to think of all the stuff that's constantly making me worry.

When I get back to the flat, luckily Zoe has finished cooking and is now sat on the couch with her legs curled up and a tray on top of her.

'Where did you go?' she asks. 'You've been a while.'

'Just out, for a walk.'

'Another one?'

'Yeah.'

'Gosh, from all this walking I bet you're losing a lot of calories. You're going to disappear into thin air.'

'That wouldn't be a bad thing.'

'Ellis, please don't say things like that.'

'Sorry,' I say.

'You seemed a lot better a year or so ago – what's brought all this back?'

'Do you remember Kim, from years ago? You met her at the concert, I think.' I don't need to be any more specific than this. Zoe knows which concert I mean. We've only ever been at one together.

Zoe nods. 'I remember.'

'Well, anyway, I saw her the other day, and since then I can't stop thinking about it. All the good and all the bad that happened.'

Zoe's eyes widen. 'Where did you see her?'

'At her house. When I was delivering pizza. She ordered pepperoni.'

'Is she alright?'

'Seems to be. But since seeing her, all those worries and memories have flooded back into my brain.'

Zoe looks at me like she's staring at a puppy begging for a home. She knows enough about my past to know that I'm hurting a lot more than she ever has, but she'll never fully understand it. No one will, except for me. I experienced every detail, the pain, but also the amazing times that were spent. It wasn't all bad – in fact, a lot of it was good – it's just that it ended, and it ended terribly.

Zoe's a good friend, but I don't actually know her all that well, even though we've lived together for a good few years now. I tend to keep to myself. I moved in simply because I couldn't live with my mam and dad for the rest of my life. (Nana had moved in with them as her house was too big and the Tories had brought in the bedroom tax so her rent was too high.) Zoe happened to have a spare room and kindly offered it me.

Five months after I moved in, Zoe heard that her uncle

THERAPY

was looking for new staff at the independent pizza company which he owned. I think she pulled a few strings.

I owe a lot to that girl. She gave me a home when I had no money, and then she got me a job, and I stayed living with her, watching her become the scientist she is now.

One time, two months after I moved in, we went out and got very drunk. I hadn't done that in a long time. When we stumbled back to the flat together, we were wrapped around each other and we kept giggling. When we made it inside, we fell on the sofa, and found ourselves kissing and ripping each other's clothes off. We ended up having sex, but the next day we both regretted it straight away. We didn't talk to each other for about three weeks, and then we realised it was getting ridiculous, so we sat down and discussed how we felt. Luckily, we came to an agreement that it was just a daft mistake, a bit of fun, but neither of us felt any real connection with one another. I didn't love her, and she didn't love me. But we had sex, so there must have been at least something. We remained friends, and that was it.

I never fell in love with anyone again in the end. I can't love as I did before. That's over for me. There was only one person out there for me to love.

HUB

The next day, I went back to the office. Kim greeted me with her large, engaging smile. She took me into a small room with pot plants displayed around a table and told me to take a seat.

She went through all the rigmarole of what was expected of volunteers. For the next few days, I was to just introduce myself and meet the staff, see what activities they set for the service users, support them and so on. Different service users came in on different days, and the place was set up like an office because they wanted their service users to be seen as part of the community.

In the past they would have called this place a day centre, but now they called it the Hub. Although they were an official business that produced printing services, they were also a place for adults with mental illnesses or disabilities to come to and socialise during the day. They also did other activities in and out of the Hub, like going to tea dances and musical workshops, and because a lot of the service users were very artistic they would let them paint, draw and do craftwork.

She made it sound a lot of fun. I gave her the forms. 'Were they easy enough to complete?' she said.

'Yes, all good.'

'Are you looking forward to working with us?'

'I certainly am.'

She smiled. 'Tell me, Ellis, what do you enjoy in your spare time?'

'Listening to music.' I shrugged.

'Well then, you will love the tea dance. Lots of music to dance to there. You must go along to tomorrow's session. Lottie is taking some of the service users. They will love your company; I am sure of it. We already have another lovely young man volunteering with us, Nathan Hargreaves. You two will get on like a house on fire. All the women fancy him, but looking at you, you'll give him a run for his money!' (Was she hitting on me?) 'Right, shall we go to the main office? Let's go and introduce you to the team.' She beamed.

We stepped out of the little room and headed down the narrow corridor. The walls had framed paintings on them that I assumed had been done by the service users. Some were very colourful pictures of the countryside and beaches, but there were also a few that were black and white and looked as if they depicted local buildings.

The main office was a very large room with desks and computers. There was a big oak table in the middle. Some of the staff and service users were working on the computers or helping to print materials off. Others were sat around the table folding the paper that was being printed and making leaflets to sell.

'Ellis!' Ben shouted. He ran up to me, grabbed my hand and shook it vigorously. Lottie ran in from a side room, looking flustered. She sighed with relief when she saw me.

'Careful now,' said Kim gently. 'We don't want Ellis's arm falling off on his first day.'

'Is he coming to work with us?' asked Ben.

Kim nodded and then Ben's eyes lit up like fireworks.

'Ben, would you give Ellis a tour of the building?' Kim requested of him.

'Ellis, follow me.' He grinned. 'I am the boss, so you must listen to everything I say.'

I couldn't help but smile. It was impossible not to. Kim's face had the same expression as mine and she winked at Lottie, who was equally amused.

'This way, Ellis,' Ben instructed impatiently.

Lottie followed Ben as he showed me around. First, he took me into the kitchen. It was a small room with an island that had a bowl on top with fruit inside, cupboards up above, and a dishwasher and sink in the corner. 'This is where we come to wash our hands before lunch or after picking our noses,' said Ben.

'Ben, give over, honestly,' said Lottie, trying to be professional even though she was laughing.

Ben opened the cupboards and showed me all the stacked-up plates that were neatly displayed. They were all colour-coded, except for one. 'Who did that?' he shouted, his face turning bright red.

'Oh, dear. Ben, try to stay calm,' said Lottie. 'Just put it where it needs to be.' She knelt close to my ear and whispered, 'He likes things to be in a certain order.'

I nodded and smiled. Ben put the plate where he thought it ought to be and then shut the cupboard doors. He shook his head as if to say, 'How could someone possibly put a plate in the wrong place?' I didn't really understand what the issue was here. I had a lot to learn. As I got to know everyone, I learned that everyone there had their unique ways, and that the Hub was not a place of judgement but a place of understanding and accepting.

When we left the kitchen, Lottie explained to me that Ben had OCD and other mental health problems, as well as having a lot of learning difficulties. She said it was hard to know when it was so-called 'challenging behaviour' and when it was just because certain parts of his brain functioned differently. Even all this time later, I'm still not sure what the difference is.

Back in the main room, Ben pointed out the large table in the centre, where the service users and staff were working hard. 'This is the table where the serious jobs happen. Lottie says this is how the business gets its money. So, we must work hard so we don't lose our day centre.'

'Yeah, but you don't do any of the work, do you?' snarled a small woman. She looked to be in her mid-fifties. She was crouched over the table, folding a leaflet incredibly neatly. She didn't look up when she spoke.

'Shut up, Edith,' said Ben.

'What did you say?' Edith snapped, her eyes finally

looking away from the paper she was folding and darting towards Ben.

'Ignore him,' said one of the other staff members.

Lottie had a little word with Ben, and then Ben shook his head and continued the tour. He introduced me to the staff and the other service users around the table. We then went over to a separate table, a smaller one in the corner, and Ben introduced me to Malcolm.

'That looks incredible,' I said, admiring his drawing, which was a very detailed black-and-white sketch of the Church of St Wilfrid. 'You're really good.'

He looked up at me and gave a nervous smile. He was a large middle-aged man with a goatee and wore small glasses. 'Thank you,' he said, and then he went back to his work.

The next room was filled to bursting with computers. 'This is where we do our work, like typing and designing.'

I nodded politely.

Ben showed us one of the fire exit doors, before leading us into the last room of the building, which was bigger than the computer room and smaller than the main room.

'This is the art room,' he said. I was confused. If this was the art room, why was Malcolm in the other room?

Neither of the people around the table in this room looked up to see who we were. I assumed they were service users, as they were all working hard on their art. One of them was a young woman who was dressed like she was ready to go to a disco. She was colouring something with brightly coloured paint that matched her clothes.

The woman who was sat next to her was as thin as the paintbrush she was using to paint. Her art was beautiful. I think it was a watercolour drawing, and it was of a beach. The water looked so real I was scared to walk any closer in case I fell in and drowned. I can't swim. Mam used to take me to lessons when I was a child, but I just couldn't keep my arms going. When I told my mam this, she said, 'Well, you keep them going alright when you're playing Nintendo.' She always did like to exaggerate.

'Ladies, this is Ellis,' said Ben. 'He's going to be working with us.'

The thin woman looked over at me first. 'Hello,' she said. 'I'm Sonia.'

Then the other looked up. 'I'm Taz, and I'm painting my favourite place in the world, Majorca. I am an artist, and I go on holiday with all the money I make from my paintings.'

That was impressive, I thought. I looked over at Lottie, who gave me a look to say, 'Don't believe everything these people say.' Her smile was full of warmth, though.

'Where's Nathan?' said Ben.

'He's in reception, sorting out Kim's computer. She said it's gone funny,' said Taz.

At that precise moment, a tall, slender young man walked in. He looked about my age, but his confident stride gave me the impression that he was slightly older. His hair was wavy and brown, with streaks of auburn like autumnal leaves, and his eyes were like two conkers resting under a golden sun. He looked a bit like Louis from One Direction, and he was certainly dressed like him. Tight red chinos and a white and blue stripy shirt. Our eyes locked onto each other as soon as he entered the room.

'Hello, I don't think we've met before?' He smiled.

'This is Ellis. He's our new volunteer,' said Lottie.

'Kim doesn't think I do enough around here?' he joked. 'It's nice to meet you, Ellis.'

'It's nice to meet you too,' I said.

He took my hand and we shook. His grip gave me a comfort I had never felt before. I didn't know why at the time, but I was going to find out very soon.

EGG

The next day started with me and my parents around the table having breakfast. Dad was having a boiled egg and soldiers, Mam was eating a bacon sandwich, and I was scoffing down a bowl of Crunchy Nut Cornflakes.

'Another day, another dollar,' said Dad, tapping his tablespoon on top of the egg to let it crack and spill yellow lava like a mini volcano. I looked at him and narrowed my eyebrows. 'What?' he said. 'Oh, I see. Yes, no dollars for you, are there, Ellis?'

'Barry, you know that volunteering is a good thing to be doing for society,' Mam said through a mouthful of bacon.

'Is it really? Then why don't you try telling that to David Cameron, Bill Gates and that bloody Virgin guy with the aeroplanes?'

'I am sure they do their bit, but anyway, they don't need to, they've got jobs,' said Mam. 'And Richard Branson has three children.'

'No, I didn't mean he was actually a virgin. And anyway, this is why Mr Bloody Cameron should go easy on this new generation. How are they supposed to get a roof over their head and make a living if all they can do is volunteer?' Dad dipped his toast inside his egg, then took a big bite.

'I will keep looking for paid work. This is just something to tick me over,' I said.

'Tick you over? Is that what they're calling masturbation these days? If that's what you do then I don't think you will be volunteering for long.'

'He means something to pass the time,' Mam snapped. 'Honestly, Barry. Stop talking and just eat your egg.' Turning to me, she said, 'Are you looking forward to going in today?'

'I am. A lot of the people there seem really nice,' I said.

'That's good,' said Mam. 'You said that you're going dancing with some of them today?'

I nodded, and then Dad looked at me as if I had turned into a pink and green rabbit. 'Dancing? You think you're on bloody *Strictly*? I thought you were working for an office. Since when have offices had people doing the tango?'

I explained to Dad what the whole job actually entailed.

'Hang on a sec, you're telling me that you're volunteering to help others to get paid work and can't get paid work yourself?'

'Yeah, I guess so,' I said, and Dad shook his head in disbelief. I quickly added, 'Well, not all of them will be paid. Anyway, I enjoyed my first day. If I do a good job, you never know, they might take me on.'

'That's the spirit, love.' Mam smiled.

'If you say so,' said Dad.

SKATEBOARD

Once I got out of the estate, I walked along the Stray. The grass stretched as far as I could see. There were cars stuck in the usual morning rush and lots of people on the paths heading in every direction, some taking their dogs for their morning walks.

I was dressed in a T-shirt and shorts. I was struggling to walk as the heat was strong, but then it was summer, so what did I expect? The last three weeks had been like this. I was just glad I didn't have to sit in a school hall anymore, answering pointless questions that disguised themselves as ways of getting me future employment. As if exams would do such a thing. I didn't think any of the people I'd met at the day centre would have done well in exams, but did it matter?

Lost in my own thoughts, I heard someone calling my name out across the wind that had finally come to fight against the scorching heat. I looked behind just as someone dashed past. It was Nathan, and as I turned back to look at him, he jumped off his skateboard, placed the deck under his left arm and walked closer to me.

'Heading to the Hub?' he asked.

I nodded, and to my surprise I blushed. He was wearing tight black jeans and a baggy tank top that showed off the muscles I didn't know he had because he was so slim. His hair was waving in the wind. Thank God this wind had arrived; I'd been worried that my clothes might have stuck to me otherwise. But I don't think Nathan would have noticed. His eyes were fixed to my face.

'Great, I am heading to the Hub as well,' he said. 'I will walk with you if that's okay?'

I nodded again.

'What's the matter, cat got your tongue?'

'No, sorry. Just tired.'

He laughed. 'Fair enough.' He smiled. He looked like he should be in a boy band.

As we walked into town, the scenery turned more urban. At least the bright and bolstering blue sky was still there, defined and undisturbed. We walked past McDonald's and the bank, then we passed the place that I will always remember as being Woolworth's. When I was a child, I insisted we went there every Saturday. I was always allowed a pick 'n' mix and a packet of Pokémon cards, as long as I cleaned my room and did my homework. I would always go for the chocolate footballs, which appealed to me even more in the winter as they would change the wrappers and turn them into chocolate pumpkins instead. Much more fun, as I hated football. Why kick a ball around a field when you could just listen to a good album?

Me and Nathan didn't say anything to each other for a while. I thought I had better say something soon, so I asked him how old he was.

'Twenty-one,' he said. Three years older than me.

'And do you sing?'

He laughed. I was unsure why he found most things I said so funny. I didn't take it to heart. He seemed to like me.

'I try,' he said. 'But I am no Freddie Mercury. I can play the guitar quite well though.'

I smiled at him. The sun was resting on his brown hair, making it look more of a caramel colour.

'What music are you into?' he asked.

'Oh, you know,' I said. 'One Direction, JLS…' I stopped talking as I could see Nathan's eyes widening. His cheeks bulged, as if someone were filling them with air or water. Then he burst out laughing.

'What's funny about that?' I said, finally. Why did he think I was so funny? I'm the least funny person I know.

'Sorry, it's just that I don't like those bands at all.'

'What do you like then?'

'I like punk rock. Well, pop punk is the more appropriate name, I suppose. It's my favourite genre. Blink-182, The Wonder Years, Simple Plan, New Found Glory, Broadway Calls… that kind of thing.'

'Oh, right,' I said. 'I've never heard of them.'

He stopped walking. He looked at me as if I'd said I had murdered a cat or a dog or a rabbit.

'You haven't heard of any of them? Right, well, I got some teaching to do. I know, I will make you a mix tape – well, a CD, but you get the picture. I will put all the bands on there that your ears should be listening to. Not this pop shit that you have been torturing them with for God knows how long.'

'Okay, you're on. I would love to hear these bands.'

He laughed, and I smiled.

'So, what brings you to the Hub?' he asked.

'I left school, girlfriend dumped me and I guess I needed to find something new to be doing with my life. What about yourself?'

'Well, I'm a loner who can't find himself a boyfriend, I have no qualifications and I had parents who wanted me out of the house. So, I did the same as you. I went to look for something to occupy myself, found out about the Hub and started working there.'

'It seems such a lovely place.'

'It can be. The service users are great, and so are Kim and Lottie. But watch out with some of the other staff.'

'What do you mean?' I said, although I wasn't really that surprised. Some of them had made me feel uncomfortable as soon as I walked through the door.

'Well, the other three, Morgan, Jane and Polly, are not very nice. A bunch of bullies. God knows how they got into care. They are the three most uncaring people I have ever come across. Then there's Irene, the receptionist – the biggest gossip I've ever met. So just watch your back if I was you.'

I was glad he'd warned me. I had already had my suspicions.

'I do hope they take me on as a paid staff member soon,' he said.

'Do you think they will?' I asked him.

'I hope so. I mean, why not? I have been there over eight months now. I do more than Morgan, Jane and Polly ever do. They just sip their teas, print the work that's been sent in and that's about it. I actually engage with the service users, get them to help me create things, design things. I try to help them gain new skills. I like to think I connect well and treat the service users with respect.'

'You do,' I said. 'I could see that when I was observing yesterday.'

'Thanks.' He smiled. He looked me up and down and grinned. I remember looking at Jessica that way when I first met her. I could sense my cheeks going red.

'I liked the way you handled things as well.' He smiled. 'You were gentle and kind, and very understanding.'

'Was I heck,' I said. 'I just stood around and said whatever came out of my mouth. You were much better working with the service users and you were definitely gentler in your approach.'

When I told him this, he just laughed at me again. 'What I like about you is that you're real. You don't patronise. I saw you yesterday. That's why the service users latched on to you so quickly. You spoke to them like you would with anybody.'

'Well, of course. Shouldn't everyone?'

'They should, but they don't,' said Nathan.

'But they are all human, just some function differently. There's nowt wrong with that. The people I met yesterday, a lot of them had amazing outlooks on life. I can't wait to meet the other service users.'

SKATEBOARD

Nathan smiled and nodded in approval. 'I think you're going to fit right in,' he said.

KETTLE

Some of the service users were already there. They had their support workers with them, giving them a helping hand with taking off their coats and placing their lunch boxes into the refrigerator.

'Nathan and Ellis!' Ben cheered. He had arrived with his mother, who looked worn out. She had a similar face to Ben's but a lot more hair. She looked like one of the hedges at the Valley Gardens.

'Hello,' she said to me. 'So, you must be Ellis. I'm Patricia, Ben's mother. Ben was telling me about you all evening.'

'Hi, nice to meet you.' I smiled.

Her smile reflected back, shining even brighter than the sun that summer. I think Ben's mother would have beaten the sun every time.

'It's lovely to meet you too,' she said. 'Are you the same age as Nathan?'

'I just turned eighteen,' I said.

KETTLE

'Gosh, what I would do to be that age again,' she said. This made me realise that although she had a young face, her eyes looked old. 'Were you and Nathan at the same school?'

'I don't think so,' I said.

'Oh. Didn't you know each other before coming to the Hub?' she asked. I shook my head. 'Ah well, I am sure you will be best of friends very soon.'

She smiled and then realised that Ben was making a cup of tea as she glanced into the kitchen. 'Ben, be careful, dear! That kettle can get very hot.' She shook her head and then laughed nervously as she dashed into the kitchen.

Lottie greeted us and then went to the kitchen to help Ben and his mother. Polly walked towards me and Nathan. 'Nathan, you can go in the computer room, continue the project you were working on with Trevor and Isaac. And you, Elvis.'

'It's Ellis.'

'Isn't that what I said?' She smirked as she looked behind at the witches, as I would grow to call them. I knew full well she'd got my name wrong on purpose. What a cow she was. The previous day, she'd told Edith off when she hadn't even done anything. Perhaps I should have said something, but it was an awkward situation for a newbie.

I looked over at Edith. She was sipping her drink in peace. Seeing me looking over at her, she smiled. I smiled back.

'Anyway, the King or not, you can go next door, help the artists out,' said Polly.

I knew she just wanted me out of the way, but I was pleased to have an excuse to avoid her. I think the reason she didn't really like me was because the first thing she'd heard the others say about me was how I was a natural at working with the service users. Lottie and Kim had praised me all day. She didn't like that one bit.

TITS

I went into the art room as instructed. Sonia and Taz were there again, and this time they were accompanied by another service user. His name was Rick, and he had these long dreadlocks. I introduced myself and he showed me what he was working on.

He had painted a naked woman with large breasts. I couldn't help but smile. He laughed and said, 'Big tits.' Sonia tutted, trying her best to ignore him.

'What?' he said. He loved the fact that he had aggravated her.

'Well, it's not exactly art, is it, Rick?'

'Isn't it? I think it is,' he said.

'No, it's not civilised. It's sexist and inappropriate. You should consider painting something like trees, a sunset or some birds.'

Rick took his paintbrush, dabbed it into some blue paint and brushed it all over the lady's breasts. 'There you are then, blue tits. Is that more along the lines of what you were talking about?'

Sonia looked over and then rolled her eyes. 'Grow up, Rick,' she said. 'You're forty-five.'

Rick could see that I was as amused as him. 'I am going dancing later,' he said to me.

'And me.' Taz smiled, looking up from her painting and towards us. 'I love dancing. I will be on *Strictly Come Dancing* soon.'

'Will you heck.' Rick chuckled.

Taz didn't seem to have taken in what Rick had said. She continued painting, humming a tune that sounded a lot like One Direction. That girl had good taste.

'Do you enjoy dancing?' Rick asked me.

'I never really gave it a go. But I am joining you this afternoon, so I am sure I will find out soon enough.'

'I look forward to it,' he said.

'Great,' I said.

I really liked Rick. He loved music, like me, but he liked stuff like Pink Floyd and Led Zeppelin. Rock music. Probably music that Nathan would have enjoyed more than my CD collection. I couldn't wait until he gave me that mix CD so I could find out what music motivated him. It would really help me work out his character. Isn't that what music is? A profile of your identity?

SUGAR

The rest of that morning I got chatting to Rick more, and also to Sonia, who I found out loved all the soaps on the television and all the celebrity gossip from her magazines. She told me about her past. She'd been in a violent relationship, then abused herself with drugs and become homeless through a gambling addiction. She told me about her social worker who she said was 'helping her out'. She didn't think much of him. I think there's a chance my eyes were starting to look like the water after Rick dabbed his paintbrush inside. Distorted and unclear.

Sonia was such a kind woman. She was a joy to listen to even though her stories were sad a lot of the time. They showed how she had become the stronger and more caring woman that she seemed to be then. I told her that if she had any worries or doubts, she could always come to me. She liked that and said we should go for a coffee sometime. With me being a volunteer and all that, I was unsure whether it was appropriate to hang out with the service users in my spare time, but I said I'd check with Kim.

Then I went to chat with Taz. We talked about how One Direction were amazing, and I told her about how me and Jessica went to see them in concert. Taz was dead jealous. She told me I was sexy and looked like the Irish one. I said thanks, and that she should go to Specsavers. I was certainly not sexy, but Jessica had thought the same about me looking like Niall. Maybe I didn't look as bad as I'd thought after all.

After lunch it was time to head for the tea dance. Lottie, Ben, me, Nathan, Rick, Taz and Edith all walked together to the other side of the town, where we entered a small community hall. Inside we joined a group of elderly people and some other people with disabilities, their support workers alongside them. Lottie kept close to Ben, and me and Nathan supported Edith and Taz. Rick was able to look after himself.

'Who's this? Not seen this face before,' said the woman who I found out later was the leader of the local dance group. I could tell she was a dancer; she had long and elastic arms and legs. She was hot as well. Beautiful blonde, and with breasts a similar size to the ones Rick had painted that morning. She was in her mid-twenties. Shit, I've only just realised. Rick was painting her.

I introduced myself to her and she said her name was Georgi. I went to sit with Nathan and Edith. There were chairs in a wide circle, leaving the centre of the room ready for the dancing.

'You and Georgi seemed to be getting friendly,' Nathan teased.

I blushed scarlet. 'Oh yeah, she seemed nice.'

Lottie waved at us. She was sat opposite with Ben. She was keeping away from us, as she knew that putting Ben near Edith would cause World War III in the hall. We all wanted to dance and have fun – well, not sure about fun. I was worried how I was going to look on the dance floor.

Once everyone arrived and the room settled down, Georgi got us all up and dancing as she led the way, helping us with our moves. We danced to party songs, like 'Agadoo' and 'Locomotion', and then some pop classics that I loved such as 'Dance with Me Tonight' by Olly Murs and 'One Thing' by One Direction.

I could see Nathan from the corner of my eye, laughing at me and rolling his eyes to the chosen music. I know what he was thinking: *Why can't we dance to some punk rock?* Nathan looked good as he danced. He had the moves. He still reminded me of Louis in looks but he danced much better, more like Aston from JLS. I wondered if he could do the same impressive backflip.

Lottie was having a whale of a time dancing along with Ben, but towards the end of the session she looked like she was going to pass out. When she passed me, she said, 'Ellis, I am in need of some chocolate and tea with six spoonfuls of sugar.'

'Aren't you diabetic?' said Rick.

'I don't care,' Lottie snapped, and she wandered off and disappeared. All the service users laughed at her with affection.

I stayed to entertain Ben. Or should I say he entertained me until Lottie came back with some helpers from the dance group, who were bringing out trays of teas and biscuits.

Everyone sat down and drank and ate, and I sat close to Lottie, who suggested that me and Nathan come for afternoon tea with her sometime if we fancied it. I said that sounded great, and that I would ask Nathan.

'Great.' She smiled, and then she sipped from her large cup of tea and sighed as she relaxed.

ROCKS

Andy can't make it today. He's usually the one that I go with to take Jessica to the hospital. He's a binman, so he has the most time off. Rochelle's usually caught up working in finance. She only has weekends off, but Jessica's appointments never seem to fall on those days. Today, though, Andy has to do jury duty and that means that Rochelle has to come. I did offer to take Jessica on my own, but Rochelle hated the idea and made sure that she was there in case I did anything that would cause an issue. I don't really know what she thinks I'd do. Not every building I go to bursts into flames.

When we get there, we sit in the waiting room. Silence hangs over our shoulders. Peaceful. It's what Jessica and I prefer. Rochelle keeps fidgeting with the rings on her fingers and taking deep sighs every now and then to fill the room with sound. The silence dissolves and I look at Jessica to see if she will react. Of course, she doesn't.

Then I look at her head. Her hair is almost gone. How

has this happened? How can the body give in like this? Why can't she fight these cells?

The day Andy told me about Jessica's cancer, I felt like everything around me was getting sucked into a black hole. Hasn't she suffered enough? She was losing her personality and now she's losing her existence altogether.

Soon we're called into the room where Jessica meets her radiographer. I remember when Andy first told me she'd being having these radiotherapy sessions, I said that I didn't think someone talking about transmission and reception of electromagnetic waves would calm her worries. Perhaps that's when Rochelle took a dislike to me.

I sit in the corner of the room. Rochelle is sat close to her daughter. Resting her hands on top of Jessica. Squeezing them tight every now and then.

The radiographer speaks gently, but I'm hardly taking in what she's saying. I just stare at Jessica, blocking out the sounds. Trying to get that silence back in my mind.

I say to her inside my head, 'Don't worry, Jess, it's all going to be okay. You're strong. You will fight this. You will get better. I know it. I have hope – you just need to make sure you have it too.'

I see her give a nod as if she can actually hear me. Then I come back to my senses and realise that perhaps she was agreeing to something her radiographer had said. Well, either way, it means that Jessica is responding. She's doing that more recently.

*

ROCKS

I have a night off from delivering pizzas and I could do with a long jaunt, so I cycle out to Brimham Rocks. If I'd passed any of my six driving tests then I could have had a car and got to this place much easier.

It's a place I came to a lot when I was young. It's filled with trees and long, sandy paths. You'd think you were in a desert, not the Yorkshire countryside. It's a great place to have a picnic, though. I associate it with innocence, fun and not overthinking.

When we were little me and my cousins, Ryan and Jenny, would come here a lot and play around with each other and climb on the rocks, acting like monsters, pretending we were indestructible. We'd chat about The Simpsons *and* Pokémon *afterwards, and try and spot the locations where they filmed one of our favourite shows at the time,* The Rottentrolls. *Once when we came here there was a whole production team filming some scenes for an episode of the upcoming series. The rocks are huge on top but are balanced on thin pillars, giving the impression they could slip and slide at any moment. It's not anything to worry about, though. Not even a hit by a double-decker bus would harm them.*

I walk around the whole place three times. Then I stop and eat the sandwiches that I brought with me. I sit on one of the flat-surfaced rocks and gaze out at the sunset. The sky turning into layers of turquoise, pink, orange and yellow. The trees turning black and contrasting with the multicoloured universe beyond.

I think about the times when things were simple. When I didn't worry about money, jobs, sex, future, death or how my life should be. Instead, I just lived the life I had, and it was amazing.

THATCHER

I was the first to arrive at Bettys Tea Rooms. I hadn't set foot inside since Nana's eightieth birthday.

A human dressed in the colours of a penguin led me to my table. I sat, waiting for the others to arrive. I couldn't afford to come here too often; the place was bloody expensive. Luckily, Lottie had said it was her little treat. It made sense, as she was getting paid, and me and Nathan were still volunteers. She said we deserved it because of how hard we worked around the office. I thought that was very kind of her, but it didn't mean I felt any better for it. I had been working there for around two months now. But whenever I was there, I just sat around and chatted to all the service users mainly. Lottie had said that this was part of the job though, the essential part that some of the other staff missed.

She'd made a point of speaking to me in private one day, in the kitchen when I'd arrived early. She'd said, 'Ellis, you do what the others don't. You connect with these people. No matter how nice the others are, they don't seem to treat the service users with the same respect you do.'

I'd told her that they were very kind words but that I wasn't sure it was quite true. 'Anyway,' I said, 'you connect with them just as much as I do.'

She just smiled, and then she said, 'You don't even see it, do you? But that's okay, it makes you even better than I thought.' She said not to let the others know, especially Nathan. She went on to say that although she thought Nathan was kind and hardworking, there was something that stood out about me. I felt bad when she said this. Nathan was a nice guy, and I didn't think I did any better than him.

As I waited, I stared at the shining silver cutlery that was spread out across my table. Then I looked over at the counter, seeing all the succulent cakes and pastries displayed elegantly, enticing me to grab a slice. Which would I go for? Swiss Chocolate Torte, Vanilla Slice or Gugelhupf Fresh Fruit Cream Heart? I could feel the saliva dripping from my lip.

'Ellis,' said a voice. I quickly snapped out of my daze and looked away from the counter. Nathan was standing close to me. He was smiling and waving a CD in front of my face.

'What's that?' I asked.

'The mix CD I promised you.'

I took hold of it. 'Thank you,' I said.

'It's a pleasure,' he said, and sat down opposite. 'Can't have you listening to any more rubbish, can we?'

His smile was sweeter than anything offered on the menu. He was dressed in tight black jeans and a pink top. Every so often, he would push back his fringe, which kept falling over one of his eyes.

'I researched the pop-punk genre,' I said.

'Oh yeah?'

'I realised I did like that genre after all. I just didn't realise it was called that.'

'Brilliant,' he said. 'So, what bands have you discovered were part of that genre?'

'McFly,' I said, 'and Busted.'

His face fell into his arms and then he looked up, shaking his head.

'What's wrong with that?' I said. I could see he wasn't impressed, yet he was still smiling and seemed to be mocking me.

'What's right with it? Well, it's better than listening to JLS or One Direction, I suppose.'

'I'm sorry,' I said.

'Don't be daft, you don't need to apologise. I'm just pulling your leg anyway. You can like what you want, but after you listen to that CD you will know what I'm talking about.'

We chatted for a while until Lottie finally arrived. 'Sorry I'm late, fellas,' she said as she flopped herself next to Nathan. 'Trying to park seems almost impossible these days.' Lottie lived in Knaresborough, just outside Harrogate.

Lottie told us that she and her husband Phillip had built their own house. They'd wanted to live in something that was completely their own. It had taken them three years to build. They'd been staying at Phillip's brother's house in the meantime, and the occasional week away at a bed and breakfast. She'd grown up in Harrogate but moved to the outskirts as she'd never liked living in the place she worked.

Soon the penguin-dressed waiter arrived and took our orders. I could see from the corner of my eye that Nathan was looking at him and checking him out. I felt a sense of anger, a red flush rushing through my veins. I wasn't sure why at the time. I mean, if Nathan fancied the waiter, did it matter as long as he was discreet about it? The waiter didn't seem to mind.

Lottie ordered a pot of tea and a scone. Nathan ordered the same, but I decided to go for a vanilla slice and a glass of cold milk. When the waiter moved away, Lottie started to talk about how wonderful it was to have two strapping lads working at the Hub and doing such a good job with the service users, making them all feel happy and satisfied with their time there at the day centre. Lottie said she'd worked in a factory when she was very young and only got into care work when she passed her forties.

'The factory was a fun time; all the staff were women. We used to make jumpers for this small independent company. Gone now. As with many things, there isn't enough money to go around anymore.'

'There is enough money,' said Nathan. 'It's just when you have the Tory government in charge, it's unlikely they will share that money with people who need it.'

'Yes, you have a point,' she said. 'Though we did have the Conservatives in charge when I was working there. But they'd only just come to power, and it was a lot more alive and relaxed before then. So yes, perhaps you're right.'

'I know I am,' said Nathan. 'It was probably Maggie Thatcher that closed that place down. I'm not saying everything they have done is bad, but they really just care about themselves. Well, so do most politicians. It's crazy. I mean, the point of their jobs is to help people get the most out of their lives. Why don't they do that? Think what we could have at the day centre if we had the money.'

'Yeah,' I said, nodding my head in agreement to make it look like I knew what I was talking about. 'The Tories led our generation to work for nothing.'

'It's a shame, I know,' said Lottie, 'but I think soon enough Kim will be paying you to work there.'

'You really think so?' I asked. She nodded determinedly. How could she have been so certain? Nathan was smiling at me, which made me a bit self-conscious. I wasn't sure whether Lottie had been speaking to us both or just to me.

'Sorry with all the politics,' said Nathan. 'I just get frustrated at times.'

'No need to apologise,' said Lottie. 'I think it's good you're speaking out. If people didn't then there certainly wouldn't be any change.'

I wanted to try to sound like I was as politically engaged as them. The last thing I'd said was only what my dad always says to me, but I wanted to say something that came from me.

'You know,' I said, 'a bird needs a left wing and a right wing to enable it to fly. So why can't the left wing and right wing of politics work together so we can make society fly?'

Lottie giggled. She couldn't stop herself. But Nathan smiled and nodded, this time with no glint of mockery. I think I had finally proven to him that I was more than what you saw on the surface. The only thing I was doing to let the side down was not liking good music. Well, what he thought was good music. I couldn't wait to hear the music off his CD and find out what made this boy tick. As soon as we finished at the tea rooms I'd be heading back home and playing the songs from start to finish. Hopefully enjoying them as much as Nathan.

I didn't know at the time why I wanted to impress Nathan so much. I mean, he was a cool guy and he was interesting. But up until this point a guy had never made me feel like this before. I knew that I liked Louis from One Direction and Aston from JLS, but that was because they had beautiful singing voices. Perhaps Nathan had a beautiful voice when he sang?

Our food soon arrived. Lottie tucked in, making satisfied groans on nearly every bite. 'I needed this!' she exclaimed.

As we came to an end of our scoffing and slurping, Lottie wiped her face, and then looked at me and Nathan with eyes that were trying to say something.

'Is everything okay?' said Nathan, slightly concerned.

Lottie sighed and then said, 'Not really.'

'Sorry, is it something I said?'

'No, don't be silly. You two are great, and today has

been absolutely lovely. Thank you for coming out to Bettys with me. I really appreciate it. It's just there's something I have been wanting to say the whole time we were here, and there hasn't been an appropriate time to say it.'

'What is it?' asked Nathan.

'Two of the staff back at the Hub, they have been bullying me.'

'Which ones?' I asked.

'Jane and Polly, but mostly Jane.'

'They are not very nice,' I said. 'I don't really like Morgan either, to be honest.'

'Lottie, they are bullies to everyone,' said Nathan. 'Have you heard some of the things they say to the service users? That's even worse.'

Lottie nodded. 'I have, and I keep telling Kim in supervision, but she just thinks I am overreacting. Of course, whenever she's in the room they don't act the same way.'

'I know,' said Nathan. 'But please don't let them get to you, Lottie. You know it's not you. It's them. They are just bullies. That's all they are. They are just jealous because they know the service users prefer us to them. Remember, you haven't done anything wrong.'

'Thank you,' Lottie said.

'What have they said or done to you?' asked Nathan.

'If I am alone in the office with them, they giggle between themselves, talking loudly to make sure I can hear. They mock the way I dress, they say I am overweight and that I let the service users get away with everything. That I don't set a good example.'

'You shouldn't worry about the way you look or dress. You look great!' I said.

'Thank you, Ellis, that's very sweet,' Lottie said, taking the last sip of her tea.

'We're not there to set an example – the service users we work with are adults,' I continued. 'We are there just to advise and support in the best possible way, and you certainly do that.'

Lottie was nodding, looking down at her cup. Her eyes were watering.

'The thing that upsets me most,' she said, 'was they mocked the way I behaved towards you two, just because I do my best to be kind to you. You see, me and Phillip, we never had a child of our own. We tried for several years, but I just wasn't able to. We did wonder if we should try adoption, but work and life just got in the way and we never found a suitable time to do it. I felt like I let Phillip down. He was always very sweet and said it wasn't my fault, but that didn't stop me thinking it was. Anyway, I see you two as the sons I never had. Especially since you arrived, Ellis… seeing the way you both click, it's wonderful, truly magical. I always wanted two boys, and now I feel I do.'

Nathan got up and gave her a huge hug. I wasn't sure what to do, so I followed his lead. People around us must have stared and wondered what on Earth we were doing. It must have looked like we were trying to build a human pyramid inside the café.

As we sat back down, I looked at Nathan. The thought of us as brothers was odd, because I didn't want to think of us as brothers. Again, I wasn't quite sure why at the time.

After Lottie paid the bill, she invited me and Nathan to her house sometime so we could meet Phillip. 'He'd love to meet you,' she said.

'It would be our pleasure,' Nathan said, and then he looked at me and smiled.

I smiled back at him. Then I looked at Lottie and gave her one last hug.

BEN

The autumnal leaves were buoyant in the wind. Crimson and auburn. The sun peeked through the clouds and warmed my body.

I was in town with Ben. Lottie had asked if I could take him out to buy some crafts, ready for Halloween. We passed people holding onto their hats, going in and out of shops. I swear people were already purchasing their Christmas presents. How ridiculous.

Ben was wrapped up warm in his woolly coat and thick scarf that resembled the colours of the Fourth Doctor. I hadn't seen him wear it before. When I asked him about it, he told me his mother had knitted it for him recently. 'Do you like *Doctor Who*?' I asked.

He looked at me and smiled. 'Yes, of course,' he said. 'Tom Baker was the best Doctor.' This made me realise that he must have grown up in the '70s. Your favourite Doctor is like your favourite music; it's always a reflection of your generation.

BEN

I told him that I loved *Doctor Who*, and we talked all about Daleks and Cybermen until we got into The Works. The first thing we saw when we got inside was a large model of Frankenstein's monster. Scattered around him were pumpkins, sweets and Halloween costumes of devils, witches and ghouls.

Ben ran up to the display and his eyes shone with glee. 'I want to buy this!' he said, picking up the costume of the devil.

'You don't need that,' I said, knowing full well that he didn't have enough money with him to get it.

'Yes, I do!' he insisted.

'No, you don't, you're scary enough as it is,' I said, trying to distract him.

'Ellis, don't be silly,' he said crossly.

'I'm not.'

'I want to buy this.'

'I don't think you have enough. You can only spend what you have.'

He put back the costume and got out his wallet from one of his pockets. He looked inside and pulled out a few coins. 'There,' he said, jostling his hands to my chest, the coins shining in my eyes.

'I'm sorry, Ben, but that isn't enough. This costume costs £15.99.'

His face started to turn red. I felt like telling him that he didn't need the costume anymore as his face was turning the same colour as the devil, but it wouldn't have been appropriate.

'You buy it for me!' he said.

'I can't,' I said. 'I only have the money Lottie gave me, and that's strictly only for buying crafts for the Hub. Now, come on. Let's go and find some and get back before they send out a search party.'

Ben didn't listen. He just snatched the costume and ran out of the door. I chased after him, trying to ignore the alarm noise coming from the shop. Ben was a surprisingly fast runner, but luckily I was able to catch up with him.

I wasn't sure what to do. I don't really think they should have let me out with him. I mean, I know they had done before, and on some occasions it was quite nice. We'd go for tea and breakfasts at Wetherspoons, and it was good as everyone there knew him, and I felt safe because he felt safe too. But then there were days like this, and this one was by far the worst. He'd put me in other challenging situations before, but nothing like this. I felt bad getting angry with him, but I was so stressed. I didn't know how the staff at the shop were going to react, or the police after they caught us.

Luckily, I didn't need to get worried. Once I got hold of the costume out of Ben's hands, I walked back to the shop and he followed me from behind. He shouted at the top of his voice, but I didn't care at that point as long as he was close by. When I got to the shop and explained to the staff, they were completely fine about it. Turned out they did all know Ben. It still didn't stop me feeling a sore sick pain in my abdomen.

Eventually he calmed down, and we did have a fun afternoon in the end as he helped me choose what arts and crafts to buy. He apologised on the way back to the Hub.

BEN

'Yes, well, just don't do that again,' I said. 'Ben, you're a good guy. Why do these things?'

He just shook his head. I looked into his eyes, and he looked back earnestly. I knew Ben got like this, and although a lot of the time he was in the wrong I knew that he never really meant it. He just seemed to have this impulse. It was like he had a hidden switch button at the back of his head making his brain get taken over and the real Ben get pushed to one side. But thankfully, the rest of the journey home the real Ben was close to me. He smiled and laughed as we sang silly songs and rhymes.

Just before we got inside the Hub, Ben stretched out his hands and gave me a hug. 'Thank you,' he said.

'What for?'

'For being my friend.'

I nearly choked. Once I was able to move again, I felt a teardrop fall from my eye. I quickly wiped it off my face and walked inside.

CORRIDOR

All the service users were sat around drinking tea. I noticed that only Lottie was accompanying them, which was odd as Morgan, Jane and Polly had been there when we left.

'Oh God, here he comes!' Edith shouted, half joking, but I also think she was partly serious. Her and Ben never got on. I thought it was because they were too similar. They both wanted things done in a certain way. Luckily, Ben was taking no notice of her right this second. He seemed in such a good mood.

I made myself and Ben a cup of tea and we sat down with the others. Lottie whispered to me that the other staff were in the room next door. 'Why?' I asked.

'They are just gossiping.'

'But they're meant to be working.'

'I know,' she sighed.

'They just left you in here with this many service users? I don't know how they get away with it.'

'Neither do I,' she said.

'It's not fair on you, and it's certainly not fair on the service users.'

'I know,' she said as she sipped her cup of tea.

I thought about this for a few moments. 'These service users could do so much more if the other staff made more effort.'

She nodded and gave me a glance that was filled with tiredness, as if she had given up complaining about the other staff. She had lost that fight years ago, in countless and meaningless staff meetings. I told her that I wished I were an actual staff member so I could share my ideas. I mean, this might have been a day centre, but it was also a place to find out what talents our service users had and how we could help them get actual jobs themselves. I hadn't really seen any of this happen so far.

Lottie said that in her whole time working here, only one person had managed to get any kind of placement, and even that was only on a voluntary basis at this day centre. She said that whenever she'd tried to find better placements, the other staff would put her down and tease her for trying. I told her that she shouldn't listen to them if what she was doing was helping the service users. She sighed and told me she knew that, but it was difficult. Kim was lovely, but as a boss she just didn't sort them out. Lottie said that Kim would put her trust in the other staff, which I privately thought was crazy.

When Lottie popped to the loo, I chatted with Ben and some of the other service users. Soon Morgan, Jane and Polly came through.

'Why are we all sitting around just drinking tea? This is a place of work,' said Polly.

I looked up from my cup and glared at her, but I don't think she noticed. She turned her back and sat down on her chair to face her computer. What a fucking joke.

'Sorry, Polly,' said Edith.

Everyone finished their drinks and got back to what they'd been doing. Taz and Sonia were helping Edith to fold some paperwork. Some service users went into the computer room or the art room, apart from Malcolm, who had his own desk where he worked on his wonderful drawings of local buildings. The detail was incredible. They looked like actual architectural designs.

As there were plenty of staff in the main room, I headed to the kitchen to wash my cup. Lottie came in behind me. 'Where is Nathan today?' she asked. 'He's not been in the last few days. Have you heard from him?'

'Yeah, I spoke to him the other night.'

'Oh, that's okay then. I just worry about him sometimes.'

'Why? He's alright, isn't he?'

Lottie looked at the floor, trying not to reach my gaze. 'Yes. It's just… well, Nathan is a lovely lad, but he's not quite volunteering in the way you are.'

'What do you mean?'

'I probably shouldn't say actually. Forget I said anything,' Lottie said awkwardly.

I thought about telling her what had happened when Ben and I were out shopping, but I decided to leave it. What was done was done. I didn't want to get Ben into any more trouble. He'd said he was sorry, and that was enough for me.

'I am going to make a move,' I said.

'Alright, love,' she said, and I gave her a hug.

I walked out of the kitchen and said goodbye to everyone. 'You're going?' said Ben.

'Only for now, I'll be back in the morning. Besides, it's nearly the end of the day.'

'Bye,' he said, and I said goodbye back to him.

I walked down the corridor, admiring all the art on the walls. I was nearly at the entrance when I bumped into Kim.

'Oh, hi, Ellis.' She smiled. 'Thanks as always for taking the time to come and work here with us.'

'That's okay,' I said. 'I love working with the service users.'

'That's so good to hear. I hope you had a good day.'

'I did,' I said.

'Bye, Ellis. Will we see you tomorrow?'

'You will.' I smiled.

As I was about to step out, something occurred to me. I turned back to face Kim. 'I love seeing the art.'

'Oh, I know, isn't it just wonderful? I can't even draw stick men, that's how bad I am. I wish I were able to create something as beautiful as they can.'

I took a deep breath. I wasn't used to doing this. 'I was thinking, I don't know if you have done this sort of thing before, but I thought it would be good if we could somehow get them displayed out in the community and perhaps sell some of them, if the service users don't mind.'

Kim paused. I could see she was thinking about it, but she had one of those faces where you never knew if she was going to be cross or smiley. Finally, she said, 'I know, why don't we have a catch-up tomorrow and we can discuss this idea further?'

'Yes, okay.' I nodded. I stepped out of the Hub and headed back home.

RICK

On my way home, I bumped into Rick and he offered to take me for a pint. As I'd left slightly early and my parents were not going to be back for a while, I thought, *What the hell?*

He took me to a pub that was not far from the Valley Gardens, with chestnut-brown tables and an old-fashioned brick fireplace.

We sat and chatted about music. He went on and on about how brilliant Pink Floyd, David Bowie and Jimi Hendrix were. He told me he played guitar himself, and that he wished he could sing and play as well as they could. He told me Jimi Hendrix could see colours in music, and I told him so could I. He was impressed. He said he wished he could, but at least hearing sounds was enough for him to feel good.

I told him that he would get along well with my dad. He liked the same music that Rick did. They could talk about *Dark Side of the Moon* all night. I told him that

Nathan had got me into a new genre of music recently, and Rick agreed that it was better for me than listening to One Direction.

I don't know why, though; One Direction had harmonies, and the perfect structure of what pop music should be. Riff, verse, chorus, riff, verse, chorus, bridge and chorus like it's a ballad, and then chorus again with the same energy as before. It's how it should be. Lyrics that are simple and defined, that talk about love and happiness in a melancholy way that brings pure deep understanding of life and how to cope. I got all of that from the songs Nathan had given me as well. I'd rather that than endless solos, and structures that don't give any impression of how long the song is going to last.

As we chatted, Rick confessed that he had feelings for Sonia, but I wasn't sure what to say. I was pretty certain she didn't see him in the same way. But then, I hadn't thought he liked her that way either, so you never know. Maybe they acted like they hated each other and wound each other up because that's what people do when they're in love but they haven't quite realised? Rick asked me to talk to her when I next saw her. I agreed that I would as I didn't want to disappoint him, but at the same time I was regretting the words as soon as they came out of my mouth. I felt I was setting him up for a pretty deep fall, as the things Sonia had said about him had showed no sign of wanting to spend time with him. But like I said, maybe it was all a façade to hide her true feelings.

Rick told me he'd had a difficult childhood. He didn't have many friends growing up. A lot more people were discriminatory back when he was little. 'It was hard to make friends,' he said. 'For some reason, a little boy in a wheelchair gave them the impression that I couldn't join in with all their running and playground games. It wasn't just my classmates that discriminated against me. They put me in classes with people who weren't on the same level as me. Just because I was in a wheelchair. They seemed to think that having a physical disability meant I had a learning disability as well. I ended up with depression. I get bad days still. It's why I attend the Hub. It helps to distract myself. Depression is a funny thing. Everyone has different outlooks on it. Some say it's developed through experiences you had as a child. I don't think so myself. I had a great life on the whole. I think the truth is that the people who get depressed are the people who understand the world better than most. They are made to think they are the ones that don't fit in, but in fact they are just the ones that see it for what it is. Nothing against those kids I was put with, but I was a lot cleverer in certain subjects, so it was very unfair.'

'I bet,' I said.

'It wasn't all doom and gloom, though. I enjoyed myself more in comprehensive school. I wasn't as badly treated there. I guess because I made an effort to show what I was capable of in primary school they realised I was better suited in other classes. I made some friends there. We spent our breaks talking about the music videos we saw on *Top of the Pops* and exchanged records with each other. It's also where I started to learn to play guitar. I had a great teacher called John Patterson. He taught me all I needed to know on a fret board.'

'That's awesome,' I said. 'I wish I could play an instrument.'

'It's never too late.' He smiled.

'Doesn't Nathan play guitar?'

'He does. He's very good at it actually. Once he brought his guitar into the Hub.'

'I might ask him to do it again.'

'No, I don't think that's wise.'

'Why?'

'Because the last time he brought it in, Ben took hold of it and broke it. It was an accident, but Nathan lost it.'

'Really, Nathan? I can't imagine that. He's so cool.'

'Yeah, well. There's perhaps a lot you still don't know about Nathan. Nice guy, but he can lose his rag quite easily. Anger management is his problem.'

I was taken aback hearing Rick say all this about Nathan. The Nathan I knew was nothing like how Rick described him. Then I remembered Lottie, that look she gave me once, indicating that I shouldn't believe everything the service users said. Some were fantasists and others just saw things in a different way. It didn't mean it was true. For all I knew, Rick couldn't play guitar well at all.

'So, what about your parents?' I asked, trying to get off the subject of Nathan. 'Are you close?'

'We were. Very close to my mum and my dad. Mum stopped working as a receptionist at a health and social care building to care for me. I felt bad about that, but it was fine. When I was in my teens, I was perfectly able to get by on my own, so she started back at work around that time. Dad was a plumber. We all got on well, and they really made an effort to make sure I had a good life. They took me to concerts and we spent the weekends going for picnics or visiting the beach. They have gone now, though. Both of them. They died the exact same date, but different years.'

'I'm sorry,' I said.

'It's fine. It's life. I'm just happy we had those moments together. It's better to have them than not having them at all. And you know, some people – people at the Hub, in fact – have been treated so badly. Take Ken, for example. Have you met Ken?'

'Yes,' I said. He came in every Thursday afternoon to play on the computer.

'Well, his parents and sister would go out shopping or on day trips without him. He was always neglected.'

'Jesus,' I said.

'Yeah. Once they went to Disneyland without him. It was during one of the hottest summers. He was locked inside the house. The windows and doors all locked from the outside. He couldn't get out. There was no one to support him to get changed, make his food or to take him out to town. Poor bugger. He even still lives with them, though he's moving out soon, I think. They're struggling to find him a place.'

I hesitated and then told Rick it was best I be getting back. I didn't really want to hear any more, as Ken was such a nice bloke. He was quiet, but always polite. He would always come in and shake my hand, offer to make me a cup of tea and say the weather was nice, even if it was hailing down with a storm. I also felt uncomfortable because I didn't think Rick should have been telling me all this. I hated to think how he knew. But I knew that Morgan, Jane and Polly would gossip about the service users at times. It might have been them that he got this information from.

I downed the rest of my drink and then told Rick it was great to chat but I must be off and I would see him again soon.

FACTUAL

Once I made it home, I went straight to my bedroom. I lay on my bed playing Nintendo. I needed a distraction. I couldn't help but think of poor old Ken. I remembered that he had a nice social worker now, so I was sure he was much better looked after.

The Legend of Zelda, *Pokémon* and *Super Mario* are truly the best three franchises in gaming out there. No debate needed, just factual.

After a couple of hours I gave up and I got my phone out to text Nathan:

Hey, stressful day, but it was good fun. Missed you, though. See you there tomorrow? X

PUMPKIN

The sky was so dark, it felt like it was still the middle of the night. Only when the occasional flash of lightning appeared could I see my whereabouts, along with the lights in some of the shop windows. I was shivering, and started to run so I could get to work quicker and not get so wet from the rain. I was dressed in a Pikachu onesie. It was my Halloween costume for the day. Kim had told me that on the closest Friday to Halloween each year, they had a buffet that Lottie and her husband prepared for the service users. They played games and put on some music towards the end of the event.

At the entrance of the Hub, I jumped at the cobwebs hanging over the door. Of course, it was just grey cotton wool. How do they make it grey? You can't buy grey cotton wool, can you? I guess they just spray-painted it or something. Impressive.

When I got inside, I ran towards the radiator and rested there until I could feel my backside getting sore.

PUMPKIN

Jane arrived and shook the rain off her umbrella. She gave me a look that reminded me of my own face when I have broccoli in my mouth and walked past me towards the main office room.

I headed to the other side of the building, which was decorated with black and orange balloons. Pumpkins, small and large, were displayed around the room on different tables and shelves. There were also more cobwebs and crafted bats hanging from the ceiling.

The service users were all sat around one of the tables waiting for the fun to begin. Ben was dressed in what looked strikingly like the outfit he had tried to steal. His mam must have got it for him. I sat next to him and he raised his hands as if about to try and strangle me. I pretended I was spooked out, and then he said, 'Don't worry, it's only me,' lifting his devil mask.

I put the palm of my hand to my chest. 'Thank goodness for that!'

I looked around the room at the others. Taz was dressed as Scary Spice, Rick was dressed as Betelgeuse, Sonia was a witch, Malcolm was a vampire, Edith was a fairy. The room was enormous, and I wondered why we never used it apart from on occasions like these. It would be great for the service users if we could perhaps bring equipment here for games. I was thinking I should suggest it to Kim, and as soon as this thought entered my mind she ran into the room dressed as a glamorous witch. I think she was trying to scare everyone, but she had the opposite effect as she made all the service users burst out laughing.

At that moment Clive approached me, wearing a

Halloween-themed waistcoat and top hat and carrying a box full of poppies. He was a middle-aged man who came to the Hub every Friday, but for some reason I'd never seemed to have much chance to chat to him. He was a walking, talking encyclopaedia. He knew the bus times inside out and he loved Eurovision.

'Hello, Ellis, will you donate for a poppy?'

'Beautiful flowers, aren't they?' I said, trying to avoid the topic.

He nodded, waiting for the answer he was hoping for.

I sighed. 'Yes, alright. I am happy to help, but I don't want to wear the poppy, if that's alright.'

'I saw something about that on a panel show. Is that because you don't care about veterans?'

'No, no, it's not that I don't care,' I said, handing some loose change over. 'It's just that I feel people wear poppies just for show, without doing anything to stop wars altogether.'

'That's interesting,' he said. His eyes filled with fascination. 'I can see your point. You're talking about the government?'

'I guess so. You see them all wearing the poppies, but in reality, they don't try to stop wars. Cameron isn't doing anything to defuse the problem for people in those situations right now.'

'A valid point,' said Clive. 'Though you have helped: you have donated to this cause. So please, for me, have a poppy.'

'Clive, I am happy I have paid, but honestly, I won't need the poppy.'

PUMPKIN

'I'll have it,' said Ben, who was listening in. Clive handed him one of the poppies.

Maxi and Isabella were there, although I didn't recognise them at first. They had white bedsheets over their bodies with two cut-out holes so they could see out of them. I assumed they were dressed as ghosts. When they came and chatted to me, I could hear their accents and that's when I realised it was them. Maxi was Irish and Isabella was Scottish, so it was easy to distinguish them from the rest of us, who spoke like Wallace and Gromit. Well, not Gromit.

Maxi and Isabella had become friends from meeting at the Hub. As outsiders, they were probably drawn together. It was a good thing that Maxi had a costume to disguise herself, because Edith couldn't stand her. Lottie said it was because Ben fancied her and Edith fancied Ben. Which I was amazed about, as whenever I saw her near him she looked like she wanted to shoot him dead. But then, maybe it did make sense. Love can be like that. It was the same with Rick and Sonia, and Helga and Arnold in that cartoon show.

Shauna had a pumpkin outfit on, which meant her whole body was larger than usual and a blinding bright orange colour. Her costume was attached with braces that went around her shoulders, and on top of her head she wore a green stalk. Shauna was louder than Dave Benson Phillips off *Get Your Own Back*. She would laugh at almost anything. She was great fun. Full of life. It seemed she was only considered disabled because she was happy.

Isaac and Trevor were in matching skeleton outfits. They were usually engrossed in the computer, so it was nice to see them engaged with each other and the rest of the group.

Ken was there as well. He was sat on a chair having a cup of tea with his social worker Kathy. She was dressed up, but he wasn't. I looked at him, feeling bad that he was probably not in fancy dress because his parents and sister hadn't put any effort in to help. They would have known it was a fancy-dress party because Kathy had said she would give them the poster that clearly stated what it was. I knew she wouldn't lie.

I chatted to as many service users as I could until Lottie arrived with a bowl full of water and apples. She darted past me, then turned back in surprise. 'Oh, hello, Ellis. I didn't recognise you there. Who have you come as?'

'Pikachu.'

'Oh, I know. Pokémon?'

I nodded. 'Who are you dressed as?' I asked.

'Can't you tell? I'm Morticia from *The Addams Family*.'

'Ah, yes, I see it now. I thought it was quite witch-esque. Any of the other staff joining us?'

'No. Jane is at the other end keeping the business side of things in check, and the other two are off sick.'

'Well, that's a relief.'

'Happy Halloween!' shouted a familiar voice. I turned. Nathan had arrived.

He was dressed as a sexy nurse, fake blood dripping down his costume. His short, tight skirt showed off his legs, which he must have waxed because I couldn't see a single hair on them. He did a provocative pose at the side of the door, kicking his leg in the air.

I looked to see everyone's reactions. I thought, *Surely this isn't appropriate?* But I suppose we were all adults, and today wasn't an ordinary working day. Everyone seemed to love his performance. All the service users were howling with laughter.

'Nice legs.' Taz giggled.

Ben was speechless for the first time since I'd known him. He got up and ran over to Nathan. 'Hello, my name is Ben, what's yours?'

'Give over, it's Nathan, you daft bat.'

'Don't be silly, you're a girl. Nathan is my friend, he's a boy.'

Nathan pulled off his long blond wig, and Ben burst out with laughter. 'Oh, Nathan, very sexy!' He laughed.

Nathan came and sat next to me as we watched the service users taking it in turns to bob for apples. 'Come as a banana?'

'It's Pikachu,' I said.

He laughed. 'I knew that really. You look cute.'

I blushed.

After bobbing for apples, we played a game that I remembered from when I was a child. My mother used to do it at my Halloween parties. I used to be friends with everyone in my class and we had them round to play games and eat ridiculous amounts of chocolate and sweets. The game was that one where you have to wear a blindfold and then your hands go inside different bowls, feel what's inside and then guess what it is you're touching. It usually feels worse than it actually turns out to be.

Ben was first up, to Edith's irritation. He giggled as he placed his hand into one of the bowls.

'So, what do you think it could be?' said Kim in a cackling voice.

He pulled his hand away. 'What's that? Eugh!' He giggled. 'It feels like a brain.'

'A brain? You've felt a brain before, have you?' She laughed. 'Have another go.'

'I don't know,' he said.

He took off his blindfold and saw that inside the bowl was scrambled egg.

'Egg? That's not scary,' he said, grabbing a handful and stuffing it in his mouth.

'Ben, you're not supposed to eat it. It's for the game,' said Kim, forgetting to do her witch voice.

After everyone who wanted a turn had had one it was time for lunch. The buffet was in the corner of the room. It was elegantly displayed with the same orange and black decorations that surrounded the walls.

There were sausage rolls, olives, hummus and small rectangular pizzas. There were also scary crisps like Monster Munch, cheese and jam sandwiches, bread rolls, fruit juice in transparent jugs, and chocolate in wrapped paper decorated with pumpkins and eyes (and some pumpkin soup for people who wanted something healthy. It was placed in a large cauldron which you could scoop out like people did with punch at a prom).

During lunch I sat next to Sonia. Lottie was with Ben

and Nathan was with a few other service users, hunched together telling ghost stories. Nathan was engaging with as many of the service users as possible, just how you should. Kim was at the other end of the room, on a different table, deep in conversation with Rick.

Sonia was giving him glares across the room, but Rick had his back to her. 'I am fed up with that man,' she said.

'Why? What's he done?' I asked.

'What hasn't he done, more like.'

'Anything in particular?'

'No, I guess not. He's just so loud and happy.'

'Nothing wrong with happy,' I said.

'Yes, there is.'

'Sonia, I've seen you happy. It's a good thing. I'm not saying you need to be happy every moment of the day, but I don't think you have to dislike happiness because it only comes once in a blue moon. You can enjoy life without always having a smile on your face.'

'Try telling Shauna that.'

'Hey, come on, that's unfair,' I said.

'I know, sorry. Anyway, Rick does always have one on his face.'

'Well, it's not a bad thing either way. That's all I am trying to say.'

'It's like he must be in love or something,' she said.

'Well, actually, it's funny you should say that.'

'What, why?'

'Because he told me the other day that he had feelings for you.'

Sonia almost choked on her sausage roll. I handed

her drink over so she could gulp it down. Once she recovered, she looked me straight in the eyes. 'Is this true?' she said.

'It is,' I replied. 'Though it's a shame because you can't stand that man.'

'Well, I wouldn't say can't stand. Anyway, he's the one that can't stand. He's in a wheelchair.' I wasn't sure if that joke was offensive or affectionate. Maybe both.

'Rick's a lovely guy,' I said. 'You just got to give him a chance.'

'I suppose,' she said. 'I thought he fancied the dance lady?'

'He said the dance lady is fit as tits, but it's you that his heart beats for.'

'How romantic and poetic,' said Sonia sarcastically. 'Sexist pig. Him, not you.'

'He's like a Shakespeare play,' I said.

'Well, if he has feelings for me, he should pluck up the courage to ask me out.'

'So, you're saying that if he asked you, you would say yes?'

'Potentially. I haven't been with a guy for twelve years. The last partner I had, he hit me black and blue.'

It was like she'd drained the colour from the room. I couldn't think of anything to say except a feeble, 'I'm sorry to hear that, Sonia.'

'It's alright, Ellis. It was a long time ago. I'm okay now.'

'You're a great woman, Sonia. I mean, all the shit you've been through, I don't know how you keep so much determination. Nothing stops you; you keep going. I always wanted to sing in a boy band, but I'm too ugly and I can't sing.'

'You're not ugly, Ellis, and I am sure you can sing.'

'Thanks, Sonia, that's very kind of you. Thank you.'

After lunch Ben got his karaoke machine out and sang a few songs. I laughed as I saw Edith across the room with her hands covering her ears. Once he'd finished, he insisted I sang. I said no until Sonia encouraged me to, and then I caved and sang 'What Makes You Beautiful' by One Direction. Nathan had a go and he was much better than me. He sang a song by one of his favourite pop-punk bands, All Time Low, and he also sang a beautiful song I'd never heard of before by Linkin Park called 'Castle of Glass'. Clive sang 'Making Your Mind up' by Bucks Fizz, Malcolm sang 'Don't Stop Me Now' by Queen, Taz sang 'Spice Up Your Life' by the Spice Girls and Rick sang 'Changes' by David Bowie.

After the karaoke, it was time for dancing. 'The Monster Mash' came on and suddenly the whole room was up. Nathan came close to me, dancing seductively and in a very comical way. I stopped and laughed, and then I joined in with everyone as we sang and danced together until it was time to go home.

SNOW

I wake up to the sound of music. Not the film, but the birds chirping outside. They probably sound sweet and spiritual – but to someone who hasn't had much sleep, they sound like the nails scraping down hard against a blackboard. I get up and thump at my window. Bits of snow fall off the windowpane. I thought the snow was gone for good, but it started again last night. The frost is glistening from the sun that's slowly emerging from behind the houses on the other side of the street.

It's a cold morning. Hopefully, now the sun has made its way back, we should soon be feeling the warmth again. The birds fly away and leave me to try to come to terms with life.

My day consists of the same old routine. I meet up with Jessica and take her out for the day. We go for an English breakfast in Wetherspoons, and it gets me reminiscing about the times I had English breakfasts at BHS or Woolworths when I went shopping with my mam and my grandmother.

I watch Jessica, her face and body still as a statue. I

have to move her arms to help her cut up her food. I talk to her about nothing. I feel guilty when I see her. She's like this because someone abused her. It wasn't me, but I can't help but think I abused Nathan. I know it's not the same, but it doesn't stop me feeling this way. The person who harmed Jessica was mean and horrible. I like to think I'm not. Nathan would lose it a bit. He would lash out when he got scared. This made me scared and so I would grab him and once he fell down to the floor. For someone else looking in, it would look like I was fighting him, but it was the complete opposite. I was protecting him from doing anything worse to himself. I held his hands so he wouldn't bite them or use them to fist the walls.

After breakfast I take Jessica for a walk. I know that music isn't for us anymore, but I try to talk about McBusted. Then I think about how Mark Hoppus from Blink-182 is on their record, and how that would have upset Nathan. I try to avoid Valley Gardens when I am with Jessica now, so I take her to the Stray. I walk with her slowly, my arms wrapped around her like the wind envelops the trees. I only go to Valley Gardens when I am on my own.

Every day, before I start work, I ride my bike to the spot that was ours. The secret area where we used to hang out. I buried half of his skateboard here like a tomb. It was his favourite place. No one bothered us here. Behind this particular hedge in the Valley Gardens, where no one knew or seemed able to reach. It was as if it were made for us, and we were the only ones that could reach through, like a barrier or some kind of dome or forcefield was keeping others away.

*

There's the bench. I sit on it as I stare at his skateboard. I think about it, and I reflect on life. I breathe deeply and take in my surroundings.

It's white everywhere. It's snowed again, like it did that year. The whiteness is beautiful, but all it is is blankness. Why is blankness something that gives us colour?

I used to cry every time I sat here and looked over at him. Now I just do nothing. I am as white and still as the snow on the ground and in the trees, and on the deck of the skateboard.

After I have done my thinking, which is something I now do a lot, I pedal back to the flat. I cycle through the roads, swirling myself in and out of the cars. Little drops of snow bustle out of the trees, as a means of escape, trying to find hope, but all that happens is they fall and melt onto coats or turn to sleet on the ground.

I wish he'd come back.

PERFORMANCE

It was almost Christmas. Like so close. Next week Saint Nicholas would be doing the rounds. I remember as a kid I used to say to my parents that was the job I wanted. It would mean I only had to work one day for the whole year and could have the rest of the year to myself doing what I enjoyed. I thought that would be the best job ever. My mother said it didn't work like that. He may have only travelled the sky in one night (which, thinking about it, doesn't sound that easy or delightful), but he would also have to work all year round writing up datasets of the lists the children sent him, with columns for the good kids and the bad kids. Mam said he may have a computer now, but the job still involves a lot of hard work. Even after all that, he has to work with the elves and make sure they design the toys and get them made in time for Christmas, and when he has nearly the whole world to work for, it doesn't leave the man very much time to rest.

Dad overheard the story my mam was telling me. He

said, 'Bugger the praise for Santa, when it's us getting the toys for Ellis from our hard-earned cash.'

After Dad left the room, muttering under his breath, 'Why should that fat jolly oaf get all the glory?', Mam knelt down and whispered in my ear. 'Ignore your dad, he's only got a thing against that man because he always put him on the naughty list.'

I giggled as my mam wiped the tear that fell from my eye. 'So, Santa is real?' I asked.

'Of course.' She smiled.

Back in the day, I would have loved to volunteer with Santa, but now I was older I was more than happy to volunteer at the day centre. Working with the service users there felt a lot like Christmas all year round. I brought joy, and so did they. I felt that the service users and I would put smiles on each other's faces in the same way as if we had been left a gift under a Christmas tree.

I started to think about poor Ken. I bet he didn't get presents from Santa Claus, and yet he was such a lovely bloke. No reason to put him on the bad list, but the rest of his family sure should have been. They probably lied to Santa by making out it was Ken and not them, and so poor Ken would have missed out.

The Hub had booked to have Christmas dinner at a restaurant in the middle of town. Kim had apologised that she couldn't get me a seat as she had booked in advance. She said that she always booked in January to make sure she got a place before anyone else, to have the cheapest discount. She said that she would most certainly put me down for the following year if I was interested. She also said that she chose a different venue each year, to make it more special for the service users. So, this strategy gave her plenty of choice where their next Christmas dinner location would be.

Luckily for Ken, his social worker made sure he was going to the Christmas meal, even though it was a right struggle as his parents and sister were very reluctant to pay for it.

The beginning of that day was kind of boring. All the people I worked with, including Nathan, would be at the meal. Mam and Dad were at work. Joel was probably at work, and even if he weren't he would be making out with his new girlfriend. So, I stayed at home and lay on my bed, my headphones on, listening to the mix CD that Nathan made for me.

After four or five songs, I needed some air. So I wandered around town and saw a hat for sale in the window of one of the charity shops. I went inside and bought it. I would give it to Ken next time I saw him. He would love it.

I got a message come through to me on my phone. It was Jessica. She was back from university. She wanted to meet me in Valley Gardens.

*

When I arrived, she was sat on a bench, wearing a long, dark and seemingly expensive coat. And she was holding a white, dainty parasol. She looked very elegant. Like a movie star, waiting for her limo to take her away. She'd always been pretty flat-chested when we were together, but now she looked like she had two balloons stuffed down her blouse. But the main thing that caught my eye was her hair. It was completely different. Long, and bleached blonde. As I walked towards her, I kept doubting if it were actually her, and thought that perhaps I'd better change direction before this poor young woman thought I was about to attack her. But then she looked over at me and smiled. She waved me over.

As I got closer, I noticed she looked older. Of course, she was, but it wasn't that long ago that I'd seen her last. She shouldn't have looked that much older. Is that what university does to you? All that partying, drinking and studying? She still looked beautiful. But for some reason she was hiding her eyes with dark shades, and she never took them off for that whole conversation. I know now why she did this, but at the time it just baffled me. I would never have thought or guessed what had happened to her.

'Hello, Ellis,' she said. She'd lost her accent.

'Hello,' I replied, as I went to sit next to her.

'Thank you for meeting me.'

'It's a pleasure,' I said. 'How's the course?'

'Not as fun as I imagined.'

'Oh, right.'

'Yes, circus life looks fun on the surface, but the reality is that it's a lot of work.' (Sounded similar to Santa Claus's occupation.) 'And some of the students on the course are more like clowns in real life than they are when they perform.' She sighed. She then put the hand that wasn't holding the parasol to her side.

'Ouch,' she said.

'All that gymnastics, is it?' I said. 'That's part of the course, right?'

She didn't say anything.

I looked out at the rainy view in front of us. She should have had an umbrella on her, not a parasol. The ducks in the pond were thoroughly enjoying themselves. The dark, dreary sky made it feel like night-time, when in fact it was the middle of the afternoon.

'What have you been up to?' she said, as she finally started to talk again.

'Lots and lots,' I said.

'Then tell me. I want to hear how you have been getting on.'

'Why?' I said. 'You don't love me, so you don't need to care.'

'I can care about you without loving you.'

'No, you can't,' I said. 'Because that's what love is, Jessica. Sexually or not. Whether it's between a boy and a girl and so forth or between a parent and a kid, or just between friends, love is caring. You should try it once in a while.'

She finally stopped gazing out at the pond and looked straight at me. I couldn't see her eyes but could tell she was cross.

'Perhaps,' she said. 'Okay, well, I do love you then. Just not in the boyfriend and girlfriend way.'

'Yes, I know,' I said. 'You made that quite clear before you left. And by the way, why are you sitting and talking in that way?'

'What way?'

'Like you're some posh totty. Is that what university does to you?'

'I don't know what you mean,' she said.

'It doesn't matter.'

'Ellis, I didn't arrange to meet you so you can dig at me,' she said. 'Just so you can tell me how life has been treating you.'

'It's been treating me well. I am volunteering at a day centre, and I am hoping soon they are going to get me paid work there. I support service users with mental health problems and learning disabilities. I've met another volunteer there, and he and I get along well. He's a really nice guy.'

'That's lovely,' she said. She seemed genuine.

I told her how he looked like Louis from One Direction and the boys in Union J. Especially the one that joined the group who was originally set out to be a solo singer.

'So, you're still into your boy bands then?' she said.

'I am, but Nathan has also got me into new music. A genre called pop-punk.'

'Like McFly?' she said.

'Yeah, but less manufactured and more passion.'

'Oh, right,' she said.

There was something odd about Jessica that day. Her lips didn't move very much. There was no expression on her face. Her shades didn't help. She could have been a robot for all I knew. She hardly spoke, and when she did it didn't feel like the old Jessica that I had always known.

PERFORMANCE

She used to be the performer in our conversations, and yet now, ironically since she'd been doing a performance course, she didn't feel like one at all. She may have been dressed like one, but her personality had been lost. She didn't seem happy or sad. She just seemed like someone going through the motions. What was up with her?

I told her more about Nathan. I told her how we met up socially, and how he was teaching me how to skateboard. I told her more about the volunteering, and then, because I was running out of things to say, I told her more about the recent music I had been getting into.

She hardly said a word. I wasn't even sure if she was listening; it was hard to tell with her shades on. She stared out at the pond. It was like she wasn't even there.

I went to grab her shades. 'What you wearing these for?' I said.

But she just grabbed my hand and said, 'Ellis, please don't grab things that don't belong to you.'

I moved back. I was surprised how cross she seemed. She looked very anxious at the same time.

'Sorry,' I said. 'I was just teasing. I didn't think it would have upset you so much.'

'Sorry,' she said. 'I'm just a little sensitive these days. Not sure why. Anyway, I've got to go. It was nice catching up with you, Ellis. Have a good Christmas. Say hi to Nathan for me.'

'Can we meet again soon?' I asked, but she had already scurried off, her head facing the ground as she walked out of Valley Gardens.

BOYS

Into the new year, I continued working at the Hub, getting to know everyone there a lot better – the service users, the staff… and Nathan. Nathan and I would meet on weekends; he'd teach me how to skateboard, and we'd talk about all the wonderful music that he was getting me into. Then I'd run home, put the CD on and lie on my bed to hear the music.

Nathan and I would sit on tree stumps or lie on the grass by the Stray or at Valley Gardens. He was so pleased that I liked the songs, and that I genuinely meant it. I truly did. I did my research into all the bands and found out that the girl who sang 'Sk8er Boi' was really fit. Nathan laughed at me when I told him, and he would tease me about it forever after. There were so many great bands on that CD he gave me. They all had crazy names like Weezer, Jimmy Eat World, Fall Out Boy. Nathan said that the lead singer of Bowling for Soup was cute and that he fancied Billie Joe Armstrong from the band Green Day.

'His eyes are melancholy in an artistic sense, and his black hair is lush.'

'Green Day – "Basket Case". Track nine.' I smiled.

'That's right.' Nathan grinned.

The music was so catchy, like One Direction, but the passion was stronger and the energy was more powerful to the gut. My heart would pump endlessly as the sounds enveloped me. I would see colours, imagery around me and stories that were so vivid I was lost in a world of creativity. It brought a sense of a belonging that made the world a more understanding place to live.

I remember asking Nathan once why he loved this music so much. He said it was home to him, that the music made him feel alive. He felt like he was a part of something when he listened to these kind of bands. I asked why he connected with it so much when, apart from Avril Lavigne, the music was all about girls and he was into boys. I still remember his face when I asked him. The smile vanished and he looked down at the grass.

'It doesn't matter that they sing about girls. The same principles are there when I think of boys,' he said. 'I get the same pleasure as you would from listening to "Sk8er Boi".'

'Have you ever had a boyfriend?' I asked. He shook his head, looking glum. 'Well then, I think I will have to help you find one.'

He looked at me and smiled. He got up and started showing off his graceful skateboarding. I stayed sitting with my legs pressed in, balancing my chin on top of my knees, and watched him closely. Nathan's iPod was next to me with the speakers connected. It was on a volume enough for us to hear, but not enough that it would annoy the people that were on the other side of the hedge.

The song that played was 'Heaven Is a Halfpipe', and I remember thinking if that were true, Nathan would be very happy there. I think I wouldn't mind that either, if it meant I could watch Nathan all day long in his happy place.

God, the song was annoying, though. It wasn't as good as all the other songs he introduced me to. It was a gentle melody that wasn't as fast and loud as the others, so perhaps it's surprising that I struggled to get into it. I'd been into pop music not that long before and I should have been more into this than the other stuff, but for some reason I wasn't. It had an irritating tune. I'd told him this once, and since then he'd been playing it more often than usual. Either he was enjoying winding me up, or he was hoping that after so many plays of this stupid song I would come to finally enjoy it as much as he did.

When it finished, another song came on. Like the last one it was stupid. When I told Nathan this, he said, 'Yeah, maybe, but they are fun and not manufactured. The art is alive in these songs, unlike your boy bands.'

I didn't agree completely with this. I told him that some boy bands' songs did mean something – although I was slightly unsure myself, because David Cameron had been in One Direction's latest video and my dad said that was 'stooping to the lowest common denominator'.

'You should at least give McFly and Busted a chance. They are great,' I said. I was also going to tell him that

BOYS

even if the bands he loved hadn't been manufactured initially they had become so now. But I decided to leave it and keep those feelings to myself.

He stopped skating and came and sat by me. I thought I had upset him at first, but he didn't seem upset. I think he just needed a rest from all that skating. Nathan had asthma, so he wasn't really supposed to be skating at all, but he didn't seem to care.

'God, you love them, don't you? Look… you're right, Busted are okay, I suppose. But McFly, seriously?' He paused, and then said, 'They are hot though. Extremely hot. Are you sure that's not why you like them?'

I blushed. 'No, they have great songs.'

'If you say so,' he said.

Then he got up and started doing a strange dance to the song that was playing in the background.

SONIA

We met up one afternoon after work. I bought us a coffee and hot chocolate. Sonia chose a table in the corner of the room where there were two large, comfy sofas.

The place she'd chosen to sit was up against a large window. She was gazing out and watching the people go past until I arrived with our drinks. I put them down on the small table next to us.

'Thanks, love,' she said.

'Not a problem.' I smiled.

'People always on the move,' she said.

'That's true.'

'You know what I think?' she said. 'People on the move have demons that only get washed away in natural light.'

She bent her head and grabbed one of the many plastic bags which she always carried around with her. I watched her take out a small packet of tablets and open it up so she could drop one in her coffee.

SONIA

She noticed that I was watching her in bewilderment. 'I got to take two every day – might as well have it with something nice. Helps with my migraines. These things, much better than paracetamol.'

I smiled nervously.

'Are you enjoying yourself at the Hub?' she asked.

I nodded.

'That's good,' she said. 'It's a great place for me to go. I wouldn't know what to do with myself if I hadn't been recommended to go there. It's about the only useful thing my social worker has done for me. He's bloody useless at everything else. You know, I was supposed to be moving out into my own place two years ago, and I'm still living in a dump with two drug addicts and a criminal.'

'Oh, heck,' I said. What a stupid thing to say, but I couldn't think of anything on the spot that would have been more appropriate.

'Lottie's lovely, isn't she?' said Sonia.

'Yeah, she is.'

'She's had words with my social worker, Jermaine. And she's helping me herself. She thinks she's found me somewhere. She's having a meeting with me and him soon to discuss things further.'

'That's brilliant!' I said.

'Yeah, it is. Lottie, bless her. I think she's worried because she knows I was a drug addict once myself, and she's afraid I will go down that path again from the peer pressure of my roommates. But never again will I do that.'

'That's good to hear,' I said.

'I may not quite be in a better place yet regarding

accommodation, but I am in a better place in here,' she said as she pointed to her head. 'Mentally a lot better. I go to the Hub, because that's part of the reason I am feeling a lot better about myself. It's good I can pursue my art.'

Sonia had a real talent for art. I asked her how she got into it, and she told me it was from an early age. She'd started painting the walls as her mother and stepfather couldn't afford paper. He would beat her for it, and she would scream and scream.

'Our neighbour at the time, Mary, she could tell something odd was going on. So, she phoned social services, and I was taken away to a foster home,' said Sonia. 'Mary was as poor as us, but I knew if she were my mother I would have been loved and looked after. It's not the background I came from that was bad, it was just him. My stepdad, he was horrible, and he treated my mum and me really badly. She wasn't very nice to me either. I never saw her again, I think she was taken away. But my neighbours were good to me. I used to play with the boys that were on my street at the time.

'Once I got a foster mother, I went to school, and I enjoyed my time there as I could paint on actual paper and sometimes even on canvasses. But that didn't last long as my foster mother died of a brain tumour, and I was back in the children's home for twelve years. I missed out on most of my education. I would mess around, and the school I went to after that wasn't as good and so I ran away and joined a gang, and that's when I got into drugs.

'I got arrested at least five times, but after that I realised I needed to try and sort myself out. I became mentally ill, but luckily Mary, our neighbour from years ago, found me and she put all her savings towards getting me proper help. I will always be grateful for that. Mary was great. I wish she'd taken me on, but she had enough to deal with as she worked full time and had to look after her husband who was ill, which is something I found out much later.

'Anyway, I loved art all my life, but I just haven't had much opportunity to do it, so I am glad I can now at the Hub. If Lottie gets me this house, things really will start to be picking up. All I need is a boyfriend.' Then she snorted with laughter. 'A girl can dream,' she said. 'Although to be honest with you, I am not sure a man is right for me. I think I told you, didn't I, that I had a partner once, and he beat me and all. Maybe I'm not someone who's cut out for love.'

'Everyone deserves to be loved,' I said. 'You're no exception, Sonia. You have just had rotten luck, but I am sure you will find the right person one day.'

'Thanks, love, maybe you're right. Those were dark times, but it's all in the past now. I won't let one man stop me from finding love, someone who will actually treat me with respect and care. Who knows, maybe I'll turn into a lesbian.'

'I don't think that's how it works,' I said.

She laughed and took a sip of coffee. I smiled.

'What about Rick?'

She spat out her coffee. 'Honestly, Ellis, you do pick your moments.'

'Sorry,' I said. 'You know, he is a nice guy when you get to know him.'

'I am sure he is. We'll see,' she said, as she wiped up the mess. Then she gave me a wink.

Sonia was great. All the shit she'd been through, and yet she was still working towards a future of possibility. She wouldn't have given up or let other people ruin her life. She was a decent person, and I hoped that one day she'd be with someone who would give her all the loving she deserved.

Sonia finished our get-together by updating me on everything that was happening on the soaps and reality shows she had been watching all week, then she picked up all her bags and thanked me for meeting with her and having a drink and chat. I told her it was a pleasure.

She smiled. 'I do hope as well that if I get this house, perhaps I can start finding a job and I won't have to depend on benefits for the rest of my life. That would be nice, and I can scrap these bags and buy myself a nice handbag. Wouldn't that be nice?' she said.

I nodded. 'Next time we are in the Hub, I could help you search online for one.'

'Ellis, you're a star. That's a good idea, but let's wait till the house is sorted first.'

'Of course,' I said, and then she was gone. I watched her from the window, rushing to get her bus. Absorbing the natural light.

QUEEN

The idea worked. Kim told the other staff, and of course it was only Lottie that showed any enthusiasm. I didn't care what Morgan, Jane and Polly thought though. I was just pleased that Kim had let my idea become a reality.

Hence why one day I found myself sat next to Malcolm behind a desk in a bank. It wasn't really the sort of place I'd had in mind, but it didn't matter. I was just pleased that on our desk was displayed the fabulous art from some of our service users. After I realised he had plenty of pictures of the local area and other iconic Yorkshire landmarks and buildings, I suggested making calendars with his drawings on it. I thought they would sell well. He was very fond of the idea, and we had a blast making them. Malcolm and I grew close, and I found out a lot about him during the couple of weeks we were making them. He told me he used to work in a small independent workshop making wooden toys. He was married to a woman called Clare, and I told him he'd never mentioned her before, to which he responded by pointing out I'd never asked. Fair point.

Taz, Rick, Sonia and a few of the others all had their art displayed in framed paintings, canvasses and onto mugs. Yes, mugs. They had a mug machine and no one could seem to get it working except for me. Taz had been there that morning, and the following day Rick and Sonia would be coming.

It was a good afternoon. Malcolm and I got to know each other even more. He told me he loved music as well, and his favourite band was Queen. 'That Freddie Mercury has a mighty fine voice, what a performer,' he said.

I just nodded. I liked some Queen songs, but I thought they were a bit overrated. I kept these feelings to myself. I knew if anyone knew I had my doubts about Queen, they would call me a renegade and say, 'Off with his head!' I also found out Malcolm had a good sense of humour, even though he liked to dress in suits and waistcoats. He was very into comedies such as *Fawlty Towers*, *Laurel and Hardy* and *Some Mothers Do 'Ave 'Em*. We laughed together, picking out the scenes we found the funniest.

Once we finished, I counted the money up and slid it into my bag to keep safe. Malcolm told me that he'd had a good time and thanked me for making the whole thing happen. 'I always wanted to work in a shop like this, on the front line. I liked my old job, but it got lonely at times. It was more like a factory than an actual shop. It's nice to be with the customers for a change,' he said. 'I made items to sell before, but not ones with my own drawings on, and I never got to be in the limelight, actually serving customers. I didn't think I would be able to work like this again. So, thank you,' he said. It was only a pop-up shop, not an actual shop like he seemed to think it was, but what he said made the hairs on my neck stand on end. It amazed me how the littlest things could have such an effect on people. Malcolm gave me a heart-warming smile and tilted his hat as an affectionate goodbye.

I was just pleased I was able to bring happiness in some way. It made me feel good.

KILLER

I headed back to the Hub to drop off the money with Kim. Before I left, I asked Kim if she had seen Nathan. She shook her head and told me that he hadn't been in. I didn't like to ask her but was worried that there might be something the matter. Maybe there wasn't and I was just worrying about nothing.

I walked into the centre of town and got myself some fish and chips. I found a bench outside, sat down and tucked into the food, staring out at the passers-by.

I couldn't get my mind off Nathan. He'd stopped replying to my texts, and he had stopped coming to the day centre without telling anyone why. Was he sick of me? Was I there too much, doing all the jobs that he used to do? Did he think he had no purpose there now?

I looked down, feeling sorry for myself. The smell of salt and vinegar, the view of dead leaves and the feeling of change surrounded me like an invisible bubble.

After a while, I heard my phone go off. I got it out of my pocket. I had a text from Nathan.

Hey, funny man. Can we meet in Valley Gardens?
I'm there if ur about. Nathan ;)

Without much thought, I leapt off the bench like a frog, the leftover chips thrown in every direction. I ran down the hill and through the gates. I passed flowers, trees, bushes and a water fountain.

I couldn't see Nathan anywhere. When I gave him a call, he answered quite quickly and told me he was behind the bushes opposite the tennis courts.

I walked to where he said, and when I got there he was on his skateboard, riding back and forth in a straight line.

'Hello,' I said.

He stopped what he was doing and turned to face me. 'Ellis.' He smiled. He flipped his skateboard up in the air, caught it in one hand and then he went to sit on the bench.

'You can sit down as well, you know,' he said.

'Right,' I said. I realised that for some reason, I was just staring at him like a lost cow on the main road.

I walked over and placed my bum on the cold damp wood.

'You're probably wondering why I haven't been coming in these last few days,' he said after a while.

'Yeah, I have. What's wrong?'

'Nothing.'

'Oh. Then why don't you come back?'

'I can't.'

'Why?'

There was a pause. I could hear the wind louder than ever before. It drifted like a train through the gaps in the trees. The red and brown leaves piled in front of us. There were also lots of conkers. The same rich colour as Nathan's eyes.

I turned to look at him. His eyes were glistening from the sun that peeked through the bushes. 'I have a secret,' he said.

'We all have secrets,' I replied.

'I know, but if I tell you this particular secret, I don't think you will want to hang around with me anymore.'

'Then don't tell me.'

'I want to.'

'Okay, but whatever it is, I am sure it's nowt.'

Nathan sighed. 'The thing is, I have problems. I'm not well, Ellis. You may see me and think there's nothing wrong, but there is. It's all in my stupid head. It's a killer at times.'

At first, I was unsure what he was saying, then I thought back to what Rick had said about him losing his shit over the guitar and wondered if this linked in with what Nathan was trying to tell me. 'I don't mind,' I said.

Nathan looked at me. 'You don't?'

'No, why would I?'

'I'm not sure.'

'Nathan, I like you and you're a good guy. It sounds like this secret will hurt you more than it will ever hurt me. But I am here if you ever need any help. You know, being a voluntary carer and all that.'

Nathan stood up. 'But that's exactly my point,' he said.

'What is?'

'Ellis, listen to what I am about to say. I didn't really tell the whole truth that day when we walked to the Hub together for the first time. I used to be a service user at that day centre. I was taken there because I was ill. I couldn't work in a normal job. I went to university once and I couldn't handle the stress of the amount of work I was expected to do, so then I tried to get a job when I came back to Yorkshire. I worked in a graphic design office and again I couldn't handle the pressure. I was useless. I have depression and anxiety. I also got diagnosed with bipolar. One minute I'm jumping for joy, then the next I am lying on my bed feeling completely numb. The mood changes like the flick of a switch. I am so pathetic!'

He flopped back onto the bench. There were tears pouring from his eyes.

I didn't know what to do at first. Nathan had seemed so much more stable than this, but maybe it was all for show. So, Rick was right, by the sounds of it. But I didn't mind.

I wrapped my arms around him and gave him a hug. 'It's alright,' I said. 'It's nothing to be ashamed of.'

He wiped away his tears and looked straight at me.

'You know, I think people who hurt are the people who understand this world the most and care about it the most,' I said, slightly taking what Rick had said and twisting it around.

'Thank you, that's very profound of you,' he said. 'Ellis, I don't think you know how wonderful you are.'

'Anyone would have done the same.'

He shook his head. 'That's the thing, they wouldn't. Believe me.'

'Well, I just hope you know you're a good mate and I want to help in any way I can.'

'You still want to hang out with me then?'

'Of course. I think you're a great guy, Nathan.'

'What was the name of that girlfriend who dumped you?' he asked.

'Jessica.'

'She was a fool to dump you.'

'No, she probably did the right thing. I'm an ugly fuck,' I said.

Nathan thought about this. Then he said, 'You can never be ugly if you are kind, Ellis. You must understand this world better than anyone.'

He was gazing into my eyes. I didn't know what to say, especially as I wasn't clear if he meant that he thought *I* was hurting. Or was he coming on to me? No, of course he wasn't. He was just upset and looking for some sort of comfort. He knew I liked girls anyway. But still, there was part of me that liked the fact he might have been coming on to me.

We sat in silence for a while. 'Will you come back to the Hub?' I said.

Nathan sighed, thinking about it. Eventually he said, 'I will. I'm just not feeling great right now. But yes, I will be back.'

'Great,' I said.

Later that afternoon Nathan taught me some more moves on his skateboard, and he ended up telling me all about his dreams. How ever since he was little, he'd always wanted to run a band promotion business. How one day, he wanted to be booking three bands a month and doing concerts in different pubs and clubs around Harrogate, and that eventually, if it became successful, he would put more shows on and then hopefully book tours for bands that he would start to get to know. It was great to see him beaming as he told me.

The sun soon vanished from the sky, and Nathan and I left Valley Gardens and walked around the town centre, the street lamps guiding our way. I texted my parents to tell them I was staying out with Nathan.

Then Nathan noticed me shivering. He took off his jumper and insisted I wear it. 'Thank you for understanding,' he said. 'I'm a volunteer now, but I wasn't before.'

'I know, you said.'

He laughed and then he started to sing 'Live While We're Young'. It took me by surprise. He winked at me and laughed. 'I thought I'd best be listening to One Direction a bit more, seeing as I made you listen to my songs.'

He grabbed my hands and we started to sway. He was singing all different songs, like a medley. There was no one else about. We ended up on the floor, laughing like chipmunks. It was if we were drunk on air, or just drunk on the feeling of being wild and free. Whatever it was, it was fun.

Once we came back to our senses, we helped each other up and started to make our way home. Nathan placed his arm over my shoulder. 'You and me,' he said. 'Everything is going to be fine.'

DANCING

I'm at the Valley Gardens again. Rather than going to my usual spot, I've decided to sit opposite the large duck pond and watch a dad and his son playing with those remote controls that direct the mini boats on the water. They're so caught up in the moment that they haven't a clue that this will be a fond memory of theirs in the future.

An elderly lady with a dog is slowly coming over. She's dressed in cotton clothes and what looks like a home-knitted cardigan. As she gets closer, I can see the sign on her dog –

'PLEASE DON'T DISTRACT ME, I'M A WORKING GUIDE DOG'.

She pauses by my bench, about to take a seat. I don't want to alert her to my presence. I shuffle as quietly as I can to the opposite end. She takes a seat, and the dog rests by her knees. Phew.

'Hello,' *she says, looking right at me.*

I jump, but manage a, 'Hi, you alright?'

'Yes, I am quite well. Thank you for asking. You sound young, are you young?'

'I guess so, I'm twenty-five.'

'Oh my, you have your whole life ahead of you. You lucky, lucky thing.'

The dog is staring at me. It's a German shepherd, which intrigues me. I've only ever seen Labradors as guide dogs before. Its eyes look profound and bonkers at the same time. Its dark brown fur looks soft as silk.

'His name is Edward Jones,' says the old lady. How did she know I was looking at him?

'Lovely name,' I say.

'Named him after my husband. He behaves a lot better than he did,' she jokes. 'God, I miss him, though. He died eight years ago, and yet it only feels like yesterday when I saw him flat out on the patio with his hand held tight to the hose.'

'I'm so sorry.'

'Don't be daft. These things happen. It's nobody's fault. At least he died doing what he loved best. Watering his little garden. He grew the most beautiful flowers, you know. I told him he should have applied for the Chelsea Flower Show. He said he wasn't posh enough for that nonsense, that his garden was a place of sanctuary and not a place to show off and cause a fuss.'

'He sounded like he knew what he stood for.'

'He did.'

I stare at her face. I'm sure I recognise her.

'Have we met before?' I say.

DANCING

'We probably have,' she says carelessly. 'I have lived in Harrogate all my life.'

'Did you used to go to the tea dance, at the community centre?'

'I did, and I still do.' She smiles.

'I stopped going.'

'Why?'

'It's complicated.'

'I understand,' she says.

'So, what brought you to that tea dance?' I ask.

'Him, Edward Jones.'

'Your dog?'

'No, me husband. We always went dancing together. Most of it was done back in the day when our legs could manage it. Then we stopped, and I got very depressed. Edward could see that, and so he found out about this little group and we went there every week until he died. I decided to keep going, as I knew that if I didn't Edward would have been disappointed in me. He told me once, during the adverts on Corrie, that if he went before me I should never stop dancing. He said, keep doing it and think of me. Then after a while, I lost my eyesight and I got depressed again. My daughter encouraged me back, though, after she got me Edward Jones the dog, and I got used to walking around town with him. It took a long time, but I got there in the end. But really you never get that used to it. I mean, some people are born blind, so they don't know any different. But I could see before, and now I can only imagine. I have three beautiful granddaughters now, and I have never seen them. It's fine; when I squeeze their little cheeks and place my *hands on their faces, I can get an idea of what I think they look like, but I will never know. But that's fine, Edward my husband didn't even know he had three granddaughters. At least I do, and I tell him every day when I visit his grave. I have to put my hand over it, like Braille, to make sure it's him. I always get it right first time. Edward the dog is very good at guiding me, aren't you?' she says as she strokes him softly on top of his head. 'I wish I could see again; I would do anything to see again, but at least I am still alive and I get by, and I still do the things I love and it's brought me a very good friend, Edward the dog. I miss Edward my husband, though.'*

I'm not really sure what to say. She's rambling a bit. She reminds me of some of the people from the Hub, like Sonia and Taz. But she seems to have blown herself out and it seems rude to say nothing, so I say, 'What did your husband do?'

'What do you mean?'

'What was his profession? Something to do with gardening?'

'No, love, that was just his hobby. He also drew and painted and wrote short stories. He was such a talented human being, but he had no job. I worked in retail, but he didn't work because he was too unwell to work. He was about to become a famous writer, you know. You know how hard it is to get into that, especially for a working-class lad like he was, but he met someone once who peered over his shoulder at a train station and saw that he was writing a story, and that person turned out to be a publisher and the story was so good it took him by surprise, so he told

Edward to send it to him when it was completed and if it ended as well as it began, he'd publish it. He couldn't believe his luck; I remember him coming into my shop and telling me. He danced around the aisles and sang, scared all the customers. But then, he became too ill and he had to back out. He'd developed an illness called ME and there was very little understanding back then, even less than there is now. I tried to help him finish the story, but I was too caught up with work and Edward was losing his motivation anyway. I don't understand how doctors can have such a lack of empathy. I mean, it was obvious that he was very ill. No one would do anything to help.'

I know exactly what she means. I have moments like this myself with Jessica, very often. 'At least he had you,' I say.

'He did. It was hard at times to look after him, but I stuck by him. We loved each other very much. Every Thursday, apart from the days he was too unwell, he would come and dance with me. He knew how much I loved to dance. But once the ME got worse, it was taking too much out of him. You see, that's what people don't understand about ME. People with it can do some things that are physical, but it takes too much out of them. It's a chronic illness.'

I see her eyes brimming.

'It sounds like you had a lot on your hands,' I say. 'It's hard to support a loved one when they get ill. It can be overwhelming. But you should be proud.'

She sighs. 'Yes, it was overwhelming at times, but I would just try to remember that he was having it a lot worse than I was. Bless him. I miss him deeply.'

'I bet he's looking down at you, and pleased you still dance.'

'I hope so,' she says. 'What's the time, anyway?'

I look at my phone. 'Just gone quarter past four.'

'We've been talking a while, haven't we? I don't even know your name.'

'It's Ellis.'

'Of course it is. I remember you now,' she says.

'You do?'

'Yes, from the tea dance. You used to come there, didn't you? With that crowd with the learning disabilities or mental health issues, or whatever it is?'

'Yes,' I say.

'I haven't heard from them in a while. But I remember when they spoke about you all the time, and it was always nice things they would say about you. They must love you; I remember hearing them saying your name with such joy. You sound like a caring human being. Are you still doing that?'

'I try,' I say, thinking of my pizza delivery shifts.

'I don't think you need to try. You're a natural.'

We look out at the pond and sit in silence for a while. Eventually I ask her name.

She says, 'It's Mary.'

I have come to understand that life isn't all about having one view on things. Humans are way more complex than that.

MAGNIFICENCE

Nathan had invited me around his uncle's place. His uncle had moved to New York for work purposes. I'd asked Nathan what his uncle did, and he had just shrugged his shoulders. 'Never thought to ask,' he said. 'He just lets me crash here whenever he's not around, which I am so grateful for. I wish I could afford my own flat, though.'

Using Google Maps, I found myself outside a small but well-looked-after house. It had its own driveway and the front door was oddly not at the front of the house. I knocked and peered over at the huge apple tree in the back garden. Although there was a bit of grass, I think most of the garden was built on gravel, and there was a ramp. Nathan must have put it there, unless his uncle loved to ride on a skateboard as well.

'Hey, funny man,' said Nathan when he opened the door. 'Come on in.'

I walked through, took off my shoes and placed my coat on the hanger. The hall was a bit of a squeeze, but

Nathan led me into the living room, which was a nice, comfortable size. There was a table in one corner of the room, carrying a vase with a bunch of multicoloured flowers inside. The other side of the room had a sofa facing a flat plasma television.

'Can I get you a cup of tea?'

'I would love one, thanks,' I said.

'Great.' He smiled. 'One sugar, two sugars or none?'

'Three,' I said.

'Three?' He laughed with an amused expression covering his face. 'Bloody hell, you must have a sweet tooth.'

Nathan was only three years older than me, but I always felt like he was much older. I still don't know what it was, but he just had a flare of confidence that made him seem like he had seen the whole world. But of course, it had only been a couple of weeks ago that he'd broken down to me about his mental health and I'd begun to see all these insecurities. I guess he had good and bad days like everyone else.

I sat on the sofa and waited for Nathan to bring me the tea. I looked around the room. The wallpaper was sleek, a light cream colour. There were picture frames on the shelves, close to a pile of books. I got up and glanced at the covers. *Spock's World*, *Imzadi*, *Federation*. Nathan's uncle must have been a *Star Trek* geek. There was even a non-fiction book about UFOs; perhaps he believed in them. In the DVD cabinet, he had *E.T.*, *The X-Files* and *Close Encounters*.

'Nice angle,' said Nathan.

I turned around and stood up. He was holding two mugs of tea. I could feel my face turning red.

'Sorry, didn't mean to embarrass you,' he said.

'It's alright,' I said.

We sat down together drinking our teas like proper Yorkshire lads. He was wearing a T-shirt that had Rancid written on it (they were track nineteen on the mix CD), and his usual black skinny jeans. I was in a pullover and joggers. Nathan thought my attire was funny. 'How old are you? Eighty-seven? You're not meant to feel the cold at your age.'

'In this weather, I would feel the cold at any age,' I said. 'There was frost on my parents' car windows this morning.'

'Oh, well, fair enough,' he teased. 'Shall I get you some goggles next time I'm in town? Just in case Aurora Borealis hits?'

'What's Aurora Borealis?' I asked.

He shook his head and laughed. 'Magical lights in the north.'

'Oh, right,' I said.

We were silent for a few moments.

'I see your uncle likes his science-fiction,' I said eventually.

'He does. So do I. So does Tom DeLonge.'

'Who?'

He looked at me as if I'd told him I had murdered someone. 'He's from Blink-182, he's track six on your mix CD.'

'"Feeling This"?' I asked.

'That's the one.'

'I love that song.'

'Me too, but I forgot to put on his other band on there. Hold on.'

Nathan got out his phone and linked it to the speakers that were on top of the DVD cabinet. He played me a song that took me to another world. A song that captured love, acceptance and the magnificence of the universe. A song that gave me hope, for the first time since Jessica had left me. I watched Nathan. His eyes were closed, as if he were meditating or in a trance of some sort.

Once the song was over, he gently opened his eyes. He looked at me with a smile. Was he sleepy, or just relaxed? I was unsure.

OIL

He took me upstairs to an attic bedroom. There was a mattress on the floor, a chair with a coat hanging off it and bean bags in each corner. Fairy lights were scattered around the beams. In one corner was a desk with a computer on.

Nathan sat on the chair close to the desk. He loaded up the computer and looked across at me. I was still standing in the doorway.

'What are you doing still standing there for? Come and sit next to me.'

'Oh right, sure.'

I walked nervously towards him and crouched.

'What are you doing?' he asked.

'It's easier for me to see the screen,' I said.

'And it will be easier for your back if you got a chair. Look behind you, grab that one.'

'The bean bag?'

'No, the chair, remove the coat and bring it over here.'

I went over and took the coat off. I placed it on the mattress and then carried the spare chair over.

'That's better,' he said as he looked at me and smiled.

He had a graphic design programme up on his screen. There was an image on it of a group of musical notes with legs, huddled together like they were at a rock concert.

'What do you think?' he asked.

'It looks incredible, what's it for?'

'I designed it.'

'You did?'

'Yup.'

'Nathan, it's brilliant. You're super talented.'

'You're too kind. So, you like it then?'

'No, I love it. What's it for?

'I have been playing around with the idea of setting up my own promotion company. Remember I told you I was thinking about it?'

'That's great. You're making your dream a reality.'

'I guess. I don't know. I feel like I am giving in to the Tories. This is what they want.'

'Who cares if it's what they want or not? The most important question is, do you want it?'

'Yeah, it would be cool. I would like to be my own boss. To be able to control when I do things. It would be a joy to work and help independent bands get recognition.'

'I would be happy to help in any way I can.'

'You would?'

'Sure.'

'Thanks, Ellis.' He smiled.

'No problem.'

'So you think it will be good to use for the logo of our promotional company?'

'Ours?' I asked.

Nathan grinned at me. 'Of course, funny man. You're definitely coming on board.'

I nodded. I felt my knee brush across his and then I felt a rollercoaster rush through my body.

He then set up a Twitter account and explained how we could use it to gain popularity and get our name out there. He said it was a good way to browse for new up-and-coming bands who'd be looking for people like us to help them on their musical journey.

'How are we going to afford all this?' I asked.

'I have savings.'

'Okay, but I suppose we could also fill out some funding application forms online. Every little helps.'

'We're not Tesco's, Ellis.'

'No, but I just mean, it's great you have savings that can get us started, but if we can get money elsewhere, it means you can keep your savings for other things in the future.'

'Such as?'

'A flat to yourself, perhaps?'

'I don't have that much. But I have enough to get a band performing at some function room of a local pub. Small steps, and we can get there.'

'Okay, and I have some savings as well. I am happy to chip in if you get stuck.'

'Thank you, Ellis. That'd be great. So, you on for it?'

'Of course. However we do it, we'll find a way.'

Nathan beamed at me. 'Well said, funny man.'

'Are we just going to be looking for bands, or should we be looking for solo singers as well?'

'I guess we could look for solo singers,' he said.

'If we found four or five that sang really well, we could try and put them together to form a boy band.'

'I don't think so,' he said. So much for my ideas.

Nathan started talking about the pubs he had in mind for our first event. Then a light bulb went off in my head. 'Wait, I have another idea.'

'What is it?'

'Why not ask Kim if we can hold one at the day centre?'

Nathan frowned. 'I'm not sure about that, Ellis.'

'But that room we had the Halloween party in would be a great venue. I bet she'd let us use it for free and all.'

'That's true, but it doesn't have all the equipment, does it?'

'Well, we can ask all the bands to bring their own gear.'

'What about the sound desk?' Nathan said sceptically. 'I don't think any of the bands would be happy to bring that.'

'Okay, well, we can think on that. We would need to find a sound technician.'

'Oh, wait, I think Lottie's husband can do that sort of thing.'

'He can?'

'Yeah, I think he works in sound.'

'Well, perfect. We can ask Lottie when we see her next,' I said.

'Didn't she want us to meet her husband?' asked Nathan.

'Yes, she did. Great! Well, let's arrange to do that, and we can kill two stones with one bird.'

'Isn't it the other way around?' He laughed.

'What do you mean?' I said.

'The saying is meant to be "kill two birds with one stone".'

'Oh yes, I think you're right. I never liked that saying, to be honest, it's animal cruelty.'

'Says the boy who I see eating ham sandwiches every lunchtime at the Hub.'

'I don't know what you're talking about. Ham comes from plants, right?' I said.

Nathan laughed. 'Come on, funny man. I think it's time I made us a snack. We've been working solid.'

We went down into the kitchen and Nathan cooked us up some burgers with salad.

'Lucky your uncle had some food left in the fridge,' I said.

'No, I brought this with me.'

'Oh, nice one,' I said.

As the burgers sizzled in the pan, Nathan seemed to have noticed me squinting.

'Everything alright?' he asked.

'Yeah, why?'

'Because you look like you're having an epileptic fit.'

'Sorry, it's just oil. It goes through me.'

'Oh, right.'

'Yeah. Strange, I know.'

'It's cool. Does that mean you don't want to have the burgers?'

'I do.'

'Okay, maybe it's best you wait in the living room, and I'll bring them in once they're ready?'

'Thanks,' I said.

HOPELESS

The burgers were grand. Nathan was a great cook, and I even started being less bothered by oil after that day. After we had eaten them, we went back to work.

Nathan googled local bands close to Harrogate. We came across some pretty terrible ones until we eventually found one that had great music that we both enjoyed. They were called Squeaky Pop Rockers. After scrolling through their social media, we clicked onto their YouTube channel and watched some of their music videos. They sounded like Yellowcard mixed with The Smiths. Was a pretty cool sound, quite original too.

'I think I've seen them perform before,' said Nathan. 'They're quite big, but probably not big enough that we can't book them.'

'Cool, shall we message them then and see if they would be interested?'

'Sure,' said Nathan, and he sent a quick direct message to their Twitter account. After he had done that, we watched a few more of their videos, and then a reply message appeared on the screen and Nathan read it out. It was from the lead singer and he said he was very interested. He said that they were doing a mini tour around England, and it would be great to finish the tour off close to home.

*

After a lot of work and planning for our event (with the odd tea and *X-Files* break), Nathan went to lie down on the mattress and I sat next to him on the bean bag. We chatted about everything. Politics, music, skateboards, Pokémon, conspiracies and television shows. Nathan told me that he would bring his acoustic guitar next time and play me some of his own songs. I told him that I would like that very much.

'Thank you for getting me into this new music,' I said. 'It's incredible.'

'No problem,' he said. 'Which one is your favourite at the moment?'

'I love "Young and Hopeless" by Good Charlotte.'

'Good choice,' he said.

He was lying back, chilled, one leg bent and the other resting across it, his hands on the back of his head. He was glancing out through the window that looked out onto the garden – though from where we were, we could only see the sky and the clouds.

I always enjoyed being with Nathan. He was a great person to be around. He didn't take life too seriously, but at the same time he cared about life more than probably anyone I ever knew. There was sometimes a profound stare when he wasn't talking or smiling. It was rare that he showed it, but when he did, I liked the guy even more. He was fun, but my God, you could tell he was longing for much more. He wanted an answer; he wanted understanding. I liked that. I suppose we're all like Nathan, but Nathan had a flare about him.

I watched him as he looked out of the window as if it were his mind and he was reflecting on what was going on inside. His hair shone. His eyes sparkled like jewels in a cave.

He turned and looked at me. He grinned. It was as if he knew what I was thinking.

'Join me if you like?'

'What?' I said.

'Room for two,' he said as he patted the side of the mattress he wasn't lying on.

'Okay,' I said.

Then it happened. Something I never would have guessed until that point. It was as if his eyes were controlling me, undressing me. I did not have to ask, as I knew what he wanted and for some reason I accepted. I took off my pullover and then my T-shirt. I gently pulled down my joggers and threw off my socks. I was left standing in just my white pants. I was nervous. It was scary, but it felt good.

'Nice.' Nathan smiled.

Then I slipped them off. My pants were lying on a stranger's attic bedroom with a man staring at my natural presence.

I walked over and I kissed Nathan. He kissed me back. Thank God, otherwise I would have felt like a right numpty. But deep down I'd known he wanted it, from day one. I just hadn't realised I wanted it as well. I like girls; I have always liked girls. Perhaps I liked boys as well. That is a thing, after all. Maybe I liked anyone who was nice to me and looked pretty and shared the same interests and made me feel like I was someone. Jessica had made me feel like that for a while, but not anymore. It was now Nathan. I was thinking, *Bloody hell, I am kissing a boy*. I took off his T-shirt, then undid the button on his jeans and pressed down the zip. I pulled his skinny jeans off him and then his pants.

We continued kissing while our hands moved around each other's bodies. Then next minute he placed his tongue inside my mouth. I jumped, but it was heaven. It was peace.

We had sex for about five minutes. It was new, but it felt amazing. Nathan seemed to know what he was doing, as if he had planned this day for most of his life.

Once the sex was over, he let me have a shower. Then I went back to rest with him on the mattress.

'What just happened?' I said.

'We had sex.' He smiled.

'Does that mean you like me?'

'I guess so.'

'Does that mean we are boyfriends?'

'No,' he said.

RACHEL

I've got into two new bands recently. Although I've mostly stopped listening to music, when I came across them I didn't mind so much. They seem to let me enjoy music again. I think Nathan would have loved them. The first one is called Waterparks. The lead singer is so sexy and his voice is incredible. They sound a bit poppy like McFly, but they're more DIY and have the punk-rock attitude that Nathan always loved.

The second one is called Neck Deep. They sing with such energy and in their music videos they skateboard, party and sing about the world.

They both started when Nathan was still here, so perhaps he already knew them, but they barely had any albums at that point.

As I listen to them I imagine a parallel universe where Nathan is still with me and Jessica is herself again. Joel and Zoe are still an item, and Nathan and I are working together, either at the Hub or on our promotional company, while in our spare time skateboarding to punk rock in Valley Gardens or playing Pokémon on Nintendo.

When the music stops, I come back to reality. I'm alone in my flat. Zoe's out on a business trip. She's on the plane now heading to America, building her career. I am lying on my bed, just in my pants. Waiting until 8pm, when I will start delivering pizzas again. So much for being a pop star or even a support worker. Just a pizza boy, and a voluntary carer for my ex-girlfriend.

Being a pizza boy isn't so bad. I get to multitask by exercising on my bike while I am en route to deliver the pizzas. I work with a nice bunch of people, and I even get a discount. I know some people in much worse positions. I just never thought my life would turn out this way.

I wanted to have a career. I wanted to be with someone. I wanted a life I was satisfied with. Instead, I'm living a life like Rachel in Friends. *But at least she got Ross if nothing else. The only friends I now have are an ex-girlfriend who doesn't even take in my existence, and Zoe, who I only know through Joel, who doesn't ever want to speak to me again. I think he's being so melodramatic. It's not my fault his relationship went to shit. I am allowed to still be friends with Zoe even if he doesn't want to be.*

I spend the rest of the afternoon watching Friends. *Rachel was so hot. She looked a bit like how Jessica used to look. Not the hair, but the face. They both had that kind smile and determination in their eyes.*

RADIO

Summer approached, and I continued helping at the day centre. Nathan was there some days. It was weird working with him now, with only the two of us knowing that we'd had sex with each other. I couldn't get the images from that day out of my head. It was such a wonderful experience. It was so spontaneous; that's what I liked about it. It was like a dream. It felt unreal, but that's what made it so good. It was magical.

I still couldn't quite believe what had happened, though. I just didn't think it was me. I'd only ever liked girls, like Jessica. Now I was getting feelings for Nathan. When he'd said that we shouldn't call each other boyfriends, I'd felt my lungs crash into my heart, leaving it to try and mould back into shape. Then, when I was heading back home, I realised that it was a bit too soon, but maybe, if I played my cards right, he would soon come around to accepting that's what we were becoming. So, whenever we met, I didn't say anything about it, but I did always smile and have a laugh in his company. He was pleased, I think, that there wasn't anything strange between us. We still met up and skateboarded around town and the Valley Gardens. I even bought my own skateboard so we didn't have to share anymore, and we chatted about music, aliens and how fish and chips was the best meal out there. We would also try and get our business going but didn't do as much as we should have. Our excuse was always that we needed to discuss some things with Lottie's husband, but Lottie kept giving us days to come and then cancelling last minute, saying she was tied up with other things.

That day I wasn't going to work as I needed to do some chores for Mam and Dad, like shopping and mowing the lawn. In the evening, I would be going to visit Lottie at her home at last, as long as she didn't cancel again.

I got dressed and went downstairs. The radio was on in the background. Dad was listening to the news and reading about it in the newspaper at the same time. I told him they both say the same thing; he popped his head out from the side and snapped to me that there were different sides of the stories. He said *The Guardian* was different to what they said on the BBC, although perhaps if he was reading *The Sun* I might have had a point.

'I know you've been buying *The Sun* for Page 3, you dirty bastard,' he added, as if he had read my mind. 'If you want to wank, then I would suggest doing it without adding to the pile of money Rupert Murdoch already has.' I blushed, as Mam was at the other side of the kitchen putting together our breakfasts.

Five minutes later, she placed bacon, sausage, beans

and some toast onto the plate that was already in front of me. I buttered the toast.

'Weekend tomorrow,' she said, sitting down next to us. 'I was thinking it would be nice for the three of us to go out on a day trip.'

'Where?' I said.

'I was thinking York.'

'That would be nice,' I said.

'What do you think, Barry?'

'Sure, why not?' said Dad, who had finally put down his paper and was eating his egg and toast.

I hadn't been to York for a long time. I think the last time I'd gone was a couple of years ago with Jessica. We loved the alleyways filled with rickety shops that reminded us of Diagon Alley in the *Harry Potter* books. I'd always wanted to be a wizard before I'd even read that story. But then I wanted to be in a boy band. I wanted to sing and dance and be adored. But the problem is, I just wasn't cut out for all that, I really wasn't. Whatever Sonia said.

After breakfast, Mam and Dad shot off as they couldn't be late for work. I listened to some One Direction music and then I made a start on the lawn. I did the shopping and then came home to clean my bedroom. Afterwards, I lay on my bed listening to McFly's *Radio:Active* album on my laptop. It's really good. I'm still not sure what Nathan had against them.

Then I stared into space thinking of that day we had sex. I thought to myself, *Am I bisexual then? I suppose I might be.* Sexuality is so confusing even if you know if you're straight or gay, but if you're both that's a whole fish filled with kettles. Did I say that phrase right? I think I did; I would be good on that gameshow... What's it called? *Phrase Catch*? No, *Catchphrase*. That's it! So, if I liked boys as well as girls, which do I go for? Well, at that point, I guess Nathan. I really liked Nathan. We had a good laugh, and we liked the same music now (well, almost); I liked all the bands he showed me, and we skateboarded and watched television shows. We were getting through his uncle's *X-Files* boxset and Nathan had even got me watching *Hollyoaks*. I thought Ellis Haines would never watch soaps and enjoy them. But in fact, it wasn't that bad. In particular I loved watching Doug and Ste. They were like One Direction, but older and sexier. Sonia loved soaps, so it gave me something to talk to her about. That was nice.

CUT

At supper, I told my parents I was off to meet Nathan and that we were going to head to see Lottie. 'It's getting dark out there, Ellis – you sure you don't want me to give you a lift?' said Mam.

'No, it's fine. We'll get the bus,' I said. 'He said I could crash at his.'

'Okay, but be careful.'

'Sandra, the boy's not a boy anymore, he's eighteen.'

'I didn't say no, did I? I just said be careful.'

'Yes, and there's no need, I am always— ow.' And before Dad could finish what he was saying he accidentally cut himself opening the apple juice carton.

'See, be careful,' she said.

My dad's bleeding thumb made my head go light and I started getting queasy.

ASTHMA

'Hello, funny man.' Nathan smiled. He was there under the bus shelter. It was raining, but not too heavily. I smiled back at Nathan and stood next to him.

'Not long till the bus should be here.' He smiled again. He looked very at ease, as if he had smoked some weed, but I knew he hadn't. It wouldn't be safe with his asthma (although that wouldn't have bothered him), but in any case, he hated drugs, as his grandfather was an addict. He'd told me once all about it, and how it broke his heart. They were so close, closer than he was to his father. He said his father never really got him, and neither did his mother.

The bus took ages to come, but I didn't really mind. There was something quite romantic about standing there in the bus shelter, looking out at the dreary view. The only light came from the street lamps.

Nathan looked at me, his eyes burning into mine. 'Did you have a good day?'

'Yeah, busy.'

'How was everyone at the Hub?'

'I didn't go.'

'Oh, right.'

'I had chores to do.'

'Like cleaning your room?' He laughed.

'Yes,' I said. 'What's funny about that?'

'Nothing, I guess. It just sounds like an eight-year-old's kind of chore. You're an adult now, Ellis. Haven't you got more adult jobs to do?'

'Adults have to clean their bedrooms too. Don't you?'

'I do, it's just the way you said it. Did you do your homework as well?'

'I haven't got any... oh. Very funny.' I gave him an affectionate nudge in the ribs.

Then the bus finally arrived. We got on and sat close to each other.

Knaresborough is known for the majestic viaduct that crosses through it. Houses all jumbled together peering out at the shimmering deep blue water and fluorescent green bushes. Little paved side paths with long, delicate paddling boats resting nearby. A beautiful place to walk around with an ice cream in one hand and someone you care dearly about wrapped in another.

In the past, me and Jessica used to come here for dates, and have ice cream or takeaway chips. We even rode the boats once, but I was more scared of the water than I'd expected, and she laughed. But she soon stopped when she realised that we'd lost track of where we were. We'd come across this area that seemed deserted. We got out of the boat and then made out under a tree. Then we eventually rang our parents to come and find us and take us home.

PONCHOS

'Oh, my goodness,' said Lottie when she saw us. 'Look at you, you're absolutely soaked. Get in quick.' The rain had become a lot heavier by the time we got off the bus.

We walked into her home. It was as cosy as I'd expected. The hall had a table filled with picture frames of her and her husband Phillip.

She took us into her lounge at first. Inside was a large flat plasma screen telly like the one at Nathan's uncle's house and a small table filled with issues of *Woman's Weekly*, *Radio Times* and *People's Friend*. The sofas and chairs were big and cheerful.

She came in with a towel and wiped us down. 'No good,' she said.

'We're fine,' I said. 'It wasn't that bad.'

'Ellis, you're soaked through, my love. Both of you, go upstairs, get out of those clothes. There are some ponchos in the airing cupboard. Get them out and put them over yourselves to preserve your modesty. Go on.'

I looked over at Nathan. He just smiled and shrugged. I guess we had no choice. We went upstairs and searched for the bathroom. Once we were inside, we got undressed. I could see Nathan watching me. I blushed and smiled.

'She must mean these,' he said, looking in the airing cupboard. He got out two large ponchos, which covered our whole bodies when we put them on. They were more like dresses. They were multicoloured and looked man-made.

When we went back downstairs, Lottie was sat at the large kitchen table, biscuits and two large mugs of hot chocolate out ready for us.

'Thank you,' we said in unison. She was such a lovely lady.

'You both look good in those ponchos.' She smiled. 'Did you leave your other clothes on the radiator?'

'Yes,' said Nathan.

'Good, don't forget to take them back with you. Phillip will join us soon; he's doing man stuff in the garage.'

I asked Lottie if the ponchos were man-made. She said, 'No, love, they're woman-made. Anything done well is made by a woman. Now go on, eat those biscuits, otherwise they will go to waste,' she said. 'I'm diabetic, and Phillip don't like them.' Then she sipped her tea, which I am sure I saw her pour sugar into.

We told Lottie about our business and what we wanted to ask Phillip about. 'Oh, I am sure he will have the answers for you.' She smiled.

Then suddenly a black cat with white patches on its

face jumped up onto the table. 'Oh, this is Minty,' she said. 'Minty, say hello to Nathan and Ellis.'

I stroked Minty and Lottie told us how she had ended up with her. 'It was only a few months back actually,' she said. 'I had another cat for six years called Apricot. She died from running into a car, the stupid thing. I buried her in the grave next to my parents. I know some people may think it's a strange thing to do, but I loved my Apricot – she was a darling. I wanted to bury her with my parents so I could chat to them all at the same time. I wanted my parents to finally meet Apricot and Apricot to finally meet them. Anyway, one night, I was there on a bench looking down at the graves and this cat came to lie next to me and to keep me warm. That cat was Minty, and so I invited her to come and live with me and Phillip.' Lottie was getting quite teary. 'Death, it reaches us all eventually. I don't think I know what I would do if Phillip went, or Minty. I would have no one then. But I suppose I am no spring chicken; I may be next.' She smiled. 'Sorry, not very cheery.'

I put my hand on her shoulder and smiled. 'Whatever happens, you can always come to me or Nathan. We will support you.'

'That's very kind of you, love.'

At that point, we met Phillip. He was largely built and had no hair on top, just around his face. He had kind eyes. Reminded me of Santa Claus. 'Ay up, who are these handsome men?' he said. 'You're not Lottie's toy boys I keep hearing about?' He chuckled.

'Oh, Phil, don't be foul. You chat to these lads as I go and find some more biscuits.'

Lottie's husband came and sat down opposite us, sitting in Lottie's chair. He pushed his head close to us and looked back to see if Lottie was out of earshot (which she was – we were at the dinner table and she was now far up the other end. It was a big house).

'Thanks, lads, truly,' he whispered. 'I was joking before, but I know the real reason she sees you as her two boys. We couldn't have kids, so thank you for putting up with her.'

'That's okay,' I said. 'Don't think of it like we are putting up with her – she's a great friend.'

'That's great to hear. You're Ellis, right?'

I nodded and smiled.

'So, you must be Nathan?'

Nathan reached out his hand and they shook.

'She was having hell at that place before you came along. Well, she's still having trouble there, but you two make up for it, that's for sure. She still comes home crying, but so much less than she used to. I was going to march to that place and give them a piece of my mind, but Lottie stopped me, insisting I shouldn't. She said I would only make it worse. I couldn't see why, but I listened. She knows what's best. She tells me all the wonderful things you bring to the day centre. You should be proud of yourselves, lads, well done. Now tell me, what did you want to ask me about?'

We told him all about our idea for starting up a business promoting local bands and that we were putting a list together of what we might need – a sound technician being one of the things we needed to look into. We also mentioned that the Hub could be a good place to put on our first show.

He told us that he was happy to do it for free for our first concert. This was a great relief as the band were asking for quite a lot, but we didn't want to reject them as we knew they would bring a following. Phillip said that after that, we could see how much money we had, and if possible, we could book music venues which had resident sound technicians.

We thanked Phillip and then he said, 'No problem at all, it's the least I could do seeing as how good you are to my Lottie.'

By this point Lottie had arrived, handing Phillip a cup of tea and putting out some more biscuits for me and Nathan. She sat down close to her husband. 'So, you think you can help the boys?'

'Most certainly,' he said.

'Great.' She smiled.

Lottie and Phillip ended the evening with them telling us about their crazy camping holiday three years ago and the story behind building their own house from scratch. The house we were all sitting under the roof of. *Impressive*, I thought. I couldn't even put together a set of Lego.

Before we left, we put our clothes back on, which luckily were a lot drier. 'You shouldn't get a cold now,' said Lottie. 'Are you alright getting back?'

'Yeah, we will be fine,' said Nathan.

'Alright, well, you take care, both of you.' She beamed as she waved us goodbye from her front door. 'Bye, thank you for your company.'

Luckily, when we got to the bus stop the bus had already pulled up. We ran towards it and then made our way back to Nathan's uncle's house for the night.

AUNTY

'Ellis!' she shouts. I look over, and she's waving her hands around as if they're wings that are about to transport her to the sky.

The woman waving me over is dressed in all leather. She looks like a member of a bike gang. It's Aunty Mel. I haven't seen her in years, even though she lives in the same town. I cross the road to greet her.

'Well, well, well,' she says. 'Fancy seeing you. You would think we lived in different parts of the world, wouldn't you?'

'It's good to see you, Aunty Mel. Sorry I haven't been in touch. I have just been busy.'

'God, you sound just like your mother. Whenever I ring, she's like, "Love to catch up but I am extremely busy." I am sorry, love, but everyone is busy. You still got to make an effort to fit in seeing your loved ones. Perhaps you all don't love me.'

'Don't be silly,' I say awkwardly.

'Then come with me, and let's have a pint. I'll pay. Or

are you too bzz-say?' That's how she talks. I have no idea why.

'No, go on then. Let's have a pint.' I smile, hoping it won't be too long. It's late in the afternoon; Jessica and I stayed out longer than normal, and anyway, I didn't get much sleep last night.

*

She takes me to The Lazy Zebra, her local where she goes and drinks every evening after work, that's what she says. She seems proud, doesn't seem at all embarrassed. Fair enough. As long as she's happy and looks after herself in between. She works in a pharmacy, I think. My mam and her sisters all ended up in jobs that helped people with illnesses in some shape or form.

Aunty Mel sits down close to me and hands over a pint of beer that's filled up to the brim, the alcohol slipping down the glass and onto my hands. I lick the glass and my fingers and then sip the top so it isn't spilling out all over the place.

It's a nice cosy pub. Not many people are inside. A couple of older gentlemen are sat on stools close to the bar. There are a couple of young guys playing snooker in the corner and two ladies are chatting to each other over a traditional cooked dinner.

'Do you ever get in touch with Ryan or Jenny?' she asks.

Ryan and Jenny are Aunty Mel's children, who are, of course, also my cousins, the ones I spent my whole childhood having fun with. The simple days. I loved those days. I didn't have to worry about identity back then. I just had a laugh.

AUNTY

I tell Aunty Mel that they don't keep in touch. She asks me if I've tried. I tell her that I haven't. I'd like to, but I am just—

'Busy,' she says, finishing my sentence. 'So are they. They hardly come to visit me, you know. It makes me sad. I get people have lives, but at the same time, you should still find time for the ones you love, especially if you're the one who has given them their life in the first place. I am their mother, for goodness' sake. I raised them. I have given them food and water. Sometimes Sunny Delight before it was taken off the market for making everyone turn orange, and this is how they repay me. Was I not a good mother to them?'

'Of course you were,' I say. I hate having conversations like this, especially as I know why they went their separate ways. 'Don't put the blame on yourself just because they aren't making an effort. I know I am not one to talk about making an effort but—'

'I follow them on Facebook, though,' she interrupts. 'You're not on Facebook anymore, are you, Ellis?'

I shake my head. 'No,' I say.

'Well, they are, and I follow them on there to see what they're up to. I do ring them occasionally, but they never want to chat for long. I am proud of them both, though. You know what they're up to these days, do you, Ellis?'

'No, what?' I say.

'Ryan has got a child. You surely know about that?'

'No,' I say.

'Bloody hell, when did our family get so distant from one another? Anyway, him and his girlfriend Sheridan have got a baby girl called Poppy.'

'That's a lovely name,' I say, although privately it makes me think of pop music.

'And as well as all that, he's been promoted in his job at Barton's.'

'Great,' I say.

'Yeah. He worked himself up. Tea boy to marketing executive.'

I take a gulp of my beer, trying to hide my jealousy.

'And as for Jenny, well, she's finished a degree in... well, I can't remember what it's called. Anyway, she's become an archaeologist. Incredible. I don't know where they get their skills. I couldn't do half of what they do.'

'Don't put yourself down,' I say. 'Some people couldn't do what you do, and your job really helps the people in our society.'

'I guess so.' She shrugs. 'So, what about you, Ellis? Where are you at in your life? I remember when you were little you had all these hopes and dreams. You wanted to be a singer, didn't you? When I last spoke to your mother, she said you were volunteering somewhere, but that was at least four or five years ago now. Are you still working there? Let me guess, you're now senior member of the team. Oh, and how is Jessica? You still with her? She was a lovely girl.'

I finish my drink and march straight out of the pub. I hear her calling me back.

MASSAGE

We took the train. I listened to the album *Up All Night* all the way, but mostly the track 'I Wish'. When Harry Styles sings about how his heart feels in that pre-chorus, it gives me goosebumps.

Isn't it amazing how lyrics can bring so much understanding and reveal emotions you never knew you had? Luckily, at the time I didn't relate to the sadness of the words in the chorus, but then my mind wandered. What if Nathan had someone else? What if he was one of those people that ends up having sex with anyone they have a slight interest in? What if I was just on the side? My stomach started to turn, but that could have just been from the journey. I have never been that good at travelling. My thoughts were going at rapid speed and I was becoming more aware of the constant chug-chug-chug of the train.

I got up. Mam and Dad looked up at me with concern, but I didn't say anything. I just ran to the toilet, shut the door and threw up. When I started to feel a bit better, I wiped the sick off with the paper towels and looked in the mirror. I was starting to realise that being a close friend to Nathan wasn't enough, especially when I'd let him have sex with me. I wanted to be more than that. I wanted someone to love me. Although all these scary thoughts were rushing past me like the trees and buildings I saw through the window on my way back to my seat, Nathan wasn't like that. I was sure of it. He wasn't like Jessica. He hadn't been with anyone, he'd said. He had always wanted to be with someone, so if he liked me enough to do it with me and I gave him the offer to be boyfriends, then why didn't he take it? What was wrong with being together?

I went back and reassured my parents that I was alright. I looked over at them and realised that they had no idea I felt like this. They had no idea that I was into boys as well as girls. Oh God, were they those homophobic parents that throw you out if they find out their only son wants to be with a boy? They might want grandchildren, for me to get married. No – thinking about it, I was sure they would be fine. And anyway, if Nathan didn't want to be my boyfriend, I wasn't sure I wanted another boy anyway. Well, unless Louis from 1D or Aston from JLS asked me out. Otherwise, another girlfriend would be cool.

We arrived in York and headed out of the station and towards the town. The sun was out, and although there was a strong cold wind in the air it was a generally pleasant day. Mam was wrapped in her coat and scarf. Dad wore only a shirt, trying to be the typical Yorkshire

MASSAGE

man who didn't let the cold damage his masculinity. I was in a jumper and also had a scarf on.

We looked around the shops together and found a nice little café to have our lunch. I had a cheese and ham toastie with crisps, and then a warmed-up chocolate fudge cake. Mam had an all-day breakfast as we hadn't had time that morning. Dad had scampi and chips. Afterwards, Mam said I could have a wander around by myself while she and Dad did some shopping. She said to meet at the Minster at around 3pm.

I looked back at some of the shops we'd looked in earlier. The ones that looked like the Diagon Alley enterprises. One of the shops even had *Harry Potter* memorabilia in there. I eyed the Dumbledore wand, Chocolate Frogs and Every Flavour Beans for sale.

In the other shops there were also sweets, and there was a shop that sold weapons from fantasy films and games like *Zelda*. Now, I'm not the violent type at all, but even I thought they looked cool. If I ever got rich from the promotion company, I would have a room where I would just display all this shit. It would be amazing.

Outside there was a cute girl, quite a lot older than me. She was playing a violin and had a beret on. I chucked her a few pennies, and she glanced over at me and smiled.

'Thank you,' she said.

I blushed and then quickly walked away.

After passing the incredible York Minster, where Mam wanted me to meet her and Dad later, I found this small place on the corner advertising massage services. I thought, *Why not?* I still felt very achy from throwing up on the train, and I had some money that Mam had given me.

When I went in, I realised straight away that the place smelled strongly of incense. There were all these pieces of fabric and jewels hanging down from the door and from various walls. A Chinese woman was sitting behind the desk.

She looked up at me with a gentle and amused smile. She giggled at me.

'Hi,' I said.

'Yes?' she said. I don't think her English was that great.

'You do massage?'

She nodded. '£40 for whole massage?'

'Full body?'

'Yes,' she said. 'Money first.'

She got up, stretched out her hand and I handed over the money. 'This way,' she said.

She took me to one of the rooms, which was hidden by a long, drape-like curtain that she moved out of the way to let me in. 'Take off clothes. I will be with you shortly.'

'Thanks.' I blushed. I'd never had one of these massages before, but I just thought I needed one. The Hub was a lot of fun but could be mentally draining and it had a physical effect. That's how the aches developed.

I was unsure if I had to keep my pants on or not. I didn't know how this worked. I ended up standing with my hands close to my pants, humming and harring on what I should do. Then I heard a giggle. The woman had walked back in. I turned, and could tell my face and body were turning red.

MASSAGE

She walked up to me and tapped my bum gently. 'Off, please.' She smiled.

I nodded. It occurred to me that this may be a slightly unnecessary request, but for some reason I didn't mind. In fact, I quite liked it. I pulled off my pants slowly and rested on the massage bed.

She put a towel over my bum and started massaging me. She started on my neck, then moved to my back, arms and then legs. She was massaging higher than I'd expected. Then I felt her stroke my balls. Next minute, she pulled off the towel and started to massage my bum. It felt amazing.

After a while she asked me to turn over. I felt so embarrassed as I heard her giggle. I knew why – I had an erection.

She massaged me all over, even my balls. I looked at her and she winked. Then she gave me the happy ending I hadn't expected. I thought to myself, *Isn't this a massage parlour?*, hoping I hadn't accidentally gone into another kind of establishment instead.

Once she had finished, I got up fast, dressed quickly and thanked her as I ran out. I couldn't believe what had just happened and kept going over it in my mind.

Opposite I could see Mam and Dad waiting for me, holding a lot of shopping bags. I ran over quickly, hoping they didn't see where I'd come out from.

'Hey, Ellis,' said Mam. 'Do you want to go inside the Minster?'

'Err, yes. Why not?' I said.

After that we walked around a bit more until it was

time to head back to the train. We walked past a shop that had this wonderful display of handbags and jewellery. I turned back and placed my hands on the glass.

'What are you doing, Ellis?' asked Dad. 'Take your hands off before the shopkeeper complains.'

'I have to get that handbag, for Sonia,' I said. 'She will love it. I can give it to her closer to Christmas.'

'Okay, have you got enough?'

'Err... I think you will need to give me more money. I spent the rest.'

'Oh, Ellis, I'm not made of money. What did you spend it on?'

It was a good day on the whole. I just felt a bit of a fool.

PRIDE

When we got back home, I decided to go for a walk and arranged to meet with Nathan.

While I was out, I bumped into Ben and his mother. 'Ellis!' Ben beamed as he ran up to me.

'Hello, Ellis,' said his mother. 'You didn't come in to the Hub today?'

'No, I will be back next week. I just went to York with my parents today. What have you been up to?'

'Just shopping,' she said. 'Ben's been missing you.'

'I will be back, don't you worry.'

'Well, you take care, Ellis.'

'Will you be at the Christmas meal?' Ben asked excitedly, although that wasn't for another six months.

'I will.' I smiled.

'Yay,' said Ben. 'You can sit next to me.'

'I look forward to it,' I said.

When I got to Valley Gardens, I saw Nathan sat on a bench waiting for me. He was looking out, staring into nothingness like he did sometimes. There was a loud booming noise and chanting in the distance, so maybe he was listening to that.

'Hey,' I said as I got closer.

He looked up and smiled. 'Hey, so what you been up to?' he asked.

'Went to York.'

'Of course. What did you do?'

'Looked around the shops with Mam and Dad, had lunch with them, and then I decided to treat myself to a massage at this Chinese place.'

'Oh, nice,' he said.

'Well, it was, but I have to ask, are they supposed to massage your area?' I said, pointing to my crotch.

Nathan shook his head vigorously from side to side. Then he burst out laughing. 'I don't think so!' he said. 'Well, not in this country. Maybe it's different in China?' He burst out laughing again. 'What are you like, funny man?'

'Well, I didn't know she was going to do that,' I said.

After Nathan had stopped laughing, he asked if there was any particular reason I wanted to meet him today. I told him the truth. I asked him, if he had feelings for me, why did he have sex with me and then instantly shrug off the idea of being boyfriends?

He sighed. 'Look, don't take it personally. I do like you very much, Ellis, but I just don't think I am cut out to be boyfriend material.'

'You said you wanted someone when we first met.'

'Did I? I suppose I did. I mean… I know being gay is

getting more accepted, I just don't think I feel comfortable in myself to be walking around hand in hand, telling people, "He's my boyfriend." It's cheesy.'

'Cheesy? What's wrong with holding hands? You don't have to tell people what we are, as long as we feel tight ourselves.'

'I don't know,' said Nathan.

'Is there somebody else you're seeing?' I said.

'What? No. Ellis, seriously, mate, not cool. I am not like that.'

'I know, I'm sorry. It's just that I thought Jessica wasn't like that either, and next minute she dumps me, and then she's seeing someone else who I am damn sure she was seeing behind my back for a while before she decided to break up with me.'

'Well, I am not Jessica, alright?' he said.

'No, okay. I am sorry.'

'It's fine.'

'Well, can we still see each other and see where it goes?'

'Friends with benefits?' He laughed.

'I guess, but can we just see if we can develop it into something more?'

'Maybe,' he said. 'Is that what you want to hear?'

'It will do for now,' I said.

The loud booming noise had caught us up. A huge crowd of people were marching towards us, all in bright colours and glitter, waving flags.

'It's Pride,' said Nathan.

A topless man wearing shades was holding a large

stereo above his head. The music blaring out was my mam's favourite, 'Karma Chameleon' by Culture Club. She loved that song. Maybe she didn't mind gays after all, or bisexuals. If I had to be labelled, I guess that's what I was.

Nathan grabbed my arm, pulled me down to the crowd and we danced to the music with the others. It was a wonderful song, a hint at what the world could be if we just laughed and stopped worrying.

I looked at Nathan as we danced. Close to him were young lads, old lads, middle-aged lads, all shapes and sizes, some thin, some large, some dressed and even some twinks (a term that Nathan taught me; apparently, I came under that bracket, although I'm not entirely sure how) in pants dancing like there was no tomorrow.

But there was a tomorrow, and it wasn't as hopeful as this.

UNDERPANTS

Ben was typing a story that he said was about a superhero.
'Oh, right,' I said. 'Like Spider-Man or Superman?'

He shook his head. 'No, it's about a care worker.'

'Oh, right,' I said. 'What's the superhero called?'

'Super Ellis.'

How sweet of him. He saw me as a superhero – although I didn't know why, because I didn't do anything heroic. When I told him this he just said, 'You saved the Hub. It was boring until you came along.'

Again, this surprised me. I mean, I didn't do anything that fun with them. I did get the games room up and running in the end, although all it contained so far was a football table, board games and a karaoke – and even that could only be used at set times so the singing didn't annoy the service users and staff in other areas of the building. I didn't think many people's voices even reached that far.

I told Ben that Lottie and Nathan were fun. 'I know,' he said, 'but you're more fun.'

I smiled at him and let him carry on with his story. I was interested in where he was going with it. 'Do I get to wear my underpants over my trousers?' I asked.

Ben burst out laughing. 'No, silly,' he said.

'Oh, why not? Superman does. Do I at least get a cape?'

He nodded, still laughing at me.

I had been at the Hub most of this week. I was with Ben in the computer room today, but I'd spent plenty of time with other service users doing different activities. I'd been out one day with Malcolm, Taz and Rick doing another pop-up shop, this time at the market. That was fun, although it was bloody hot. On one of the other days, I was actually working on printing jobs in the main room, and although I hated working with service users when Morgan, Jane and Polly were about, I did my best to ignore them. Actually, they spurred me on; I would work extra hard to show them up. We folded lots of leaflets and piled them together to put in boxes ready for the delivery person to pick them up. Edith was the best at this; it was great working alongside her. She was so precise with her folding, like a human machine.

When the day ended, Ben's mother creeped up behind us and shouted, 'Boo!' I jumped out of my seat; I certainly wasn't this hero that Ben was depicting.

'Sorry, love,' she said, laughing. 'Didn't mean to frighten you that badly.'

'It's okay,' I said.

'So, what you boys been up to?'

'Ben's been typing a book.'

'Have you, Ben? What's it about?'

'It's about Ellis.' He smiled.

'Oh, how wonderful.' She beamed. 'You two are becoming such good friends.'

When I said my goodbyes to them, I went to find Lottie in the arts room and told her I was off. 'Bye then, Ellis.' She smiled. 'See you soon.'

GIRL

In the town centre, I saw Joel heading towards me. I hadn't seen him since my not-much-of-a-birthday party, which was a good year ago now. It was my nineteenth the following week. My life had changed so much, I'd almost forgotten he existed.

'Alright, mate,' I said when he reached me.

'I suppose.'

'Why, what's wrong?' I said.

'Nothing.'

'Fancy grabbing a burger?'

He paused, looking awkward. 'I don't know, Ellis,' he said eventually.

'How's the carpentering job going?' I asked, trying to be friendly. The only reason he got it was because it was his dad's business.

'Alright,' he replied. 'And it's called carpentry.'

We stood awkwardly for a few seconds. Then, 'I saw you the other day,' he said.

'What are you saying? Why are you behaving so

strangely?' I said. Joel was always a goofball, but he was acting more odd than usual.

'I saw you dancing with the gays, at Valley Gardens. Are you a gay?' he asked.

'Are you referring to the Pride march?' I said.

He nodded.

'Well, then, yes. I suppose I was.'

'Some were in just their pants, Ellis. They were dancing right close to you.'

'Joel, I don't like how you're saying all this. Talking like gays are a different species to any other human.'

'Sorry, look, I don't mind. I'm not against it. Not at all. I just didn't think you were a gay. I mean, you went out with a girl, right?'

'Joel, it's complicated,' I said, feeling very uncomfortable. 'Can we just leave it?'

'Sure. I'm just saying I don't mind, Ellis. If you like it up the bum.'

'Fucking hell, Joel. You shouldn't fucking mind. The way you're talking, it's not right.' I paused to get my breath back. That's not usually how I speak. 'Fucking hell,' I muttered again.

'Sorry, mate,' said Joel, looking a bit taken aback. 'I didn't mean to upset you.'

'Well, you have, well done.'

Next moment a girl walked towards us. She had a cute face, even though it was covered with piercings and dark lipstick. Her hair was blue, and she wore Doc Martens, stripy black and white jeans, and a waistcoat that had stars and moons on it.

Joel smiled at her and she smiled back at him. Then they locked lips.

'This is Zoe, my girlfriend,' he said after I'd watched them snog for about six minutes, like they had somehow forgotten I was there.

Zoe went to shake my hand. 'Heard a shed-load about you,' she said.

'I have heard nowt about you,' I replied.

'Ellis, don't be daft,' he said. Then he looked at Zoe, who looked a bit annoyed.

'See, I told you, Zoe, he's a joker. Of course, I told him all about you.'

'Yeah, he never stops. I was only teasing,' I said, to save the hassle for Joel.

'Remember I told you she studies plants at York University?'

I nodded, even though I didn't have a clue.

'Joel, you know it's more complicated than that,' she snapped.

'I bet,' I said.

'I also told you she loved indie music,' Joel added, desperately trying to regain credibility. 'Her favourite bands are Oasis, Franz Ferdinand and The Killers.'

'You did,' I lied.

'He told me you dig boy bands,' she said to me.

'Uh, yeah, and punk rock.'

'That's an oil-and-water sort of mixture,' she said.

'Yeah. I've recently got into all sorts, like Green Day and Blink-182.'

She laughed and said, 'That's not punk rock. Still

wicked bands, though, you get what I mean?'

Not really, I thought, but I nodded anyway. Even though she talked funny, she seemed to have more in common with me than Joel. I couldn't imagine her liking the same stuff that he did.

SHOES

Zoe's back from her work trip. She was exhausted and hardly spoke when she got in last night, but today she's going on and on about how great it was. She did talks, and also some research. Sciencey stuff that makes no sense to me, but I congratulate her, nonetheless. She insists again I should go out with her and her mates. She won't take no for an answer, she says. So I say maybe.

She frowns. 'It's to celebrate my return. You've got to come.'

In the old days Zoe would have said something along the lines of, 'It'll well totes be wicked,' or, 'Hells bells this night will be,' but she dropped that stupid slang when she reached her twenties and stopped hanging out with the likes of my old friend Joel.

This girl grew up so quickly. Her hair isn't blue anymore and she's stopped going to all the with-it shops. She looks ordinary and professional. She wears smart dresses with nice, delicate shoes. Whatever happened to ripped stockings, Doc Martens and checked shirts? Sometimes I don't think growing up is a good idea. I mean, it's good to have a mature mindset, which Zoe has, and it's what I like about her, but you shouldn't change your identity just because you want to be a well-respected scientist. Come on, scientists can be fun as well as being such clever clogs. But people change, like pretty much everything else on this planet. We are always changing.

I sigh and tell Zoe that I would love to come but I can't. She says, 'Why not?' and I feel at last I have to come clean. Tell her the truth about Jessica.

I ask Zoe if she can sit down, and she nods and sits on the sofa in our living room. She looks at me anxiously as she does this.

'Everything alright, Ellis?' she says.

I sit next to her. 'Not really,' I say.

'What's wrong?'

'It's Jessica.'

'What about her?'

'I never told you all the things that happened to her.'

The rest of the evening I tell Zoe about Jessica's abusive relationship, and how she has never been the same since. Her confidence has gone.

She met a guy on her course. That's how it all started. When she first told me about him, she never gave any sign how badly he was treating her. She never told me, in fact. It was her old school friend Melissa who told me. I remember that day like the back of my hand. I knew it had to be something serious before I even met up with her because Melissa and I were never close. She asked me to meet her outside the fish 'n' chips shop. We didn't go in. I am glad we didn't because I have fond memories of eating chip butties with Jessica when we used to go on trips to Scarborough. We'd play on the slot machines and rest on the beach, sit on top of the roofless buses, taking in the enlivening backdrop and bracing air. The chips we ate were even better than the ones in Harrogate. We went to a place called Sailor Sam's Mighty Fine Fish 'n' Chips Shop. They would give you a pot of batter on its own as an extra meal to the batter on the fish. Extraordinary.

Melissa and I walked all around town until we found a quiet spot away from the shops and under a tree. I could smell the sweet honeysuckle that was close by. She gave out a big sigh and that's when she went into detail about everything that had been happening to Jessica at university. It was so difficult to take it all in. I wanted to say to Melissa that it was all a lie, and that she was cruel to say this. But that would have been wrong of me. Melissa was doing the right thing. She was very brave to come and tell me like she did.

She told me that this guy that Jessica had been seeing was controlling towards her. Jessica had had no idea until later on when he got worse. He would lock her in her room and take away her phone. She would knock loudly on her door, but theirs was the only room on the first floor. Her roommates had stopped living there as one had left his course and the other had found a different flat early on.

I asked if she had any support from the staff at her flat or from anyone at the university. Melissa shook her head. She said that this guy Ryan (not my cousin Ryan) would lock her in but he'd still let her out eventually, and would press her against a wall saying that she must not tell anyone what he did.

SHOES

This made me have flashbacks. Those times when Jessica was behaving really strangely. Like the time I met her and she was wearing those shades and putting on that peculiar voice. She was hiding it from me. Melissa told me she only found out because one day Jessica was with her and she was in agony, and eventually Melissa got out of her what was the matter. She unfolded Jessica's jumper and lifted up the legs of her jeans. She persuaded her to take off her shades as well and she saw all the bruises and scars on Jessica's skin.

I eventually told her father all this. Jessica tried to stop me, but I had to tell him.

This is why Jessica doesn't do a lot now. It's like she's made herself numb because if she interacts with life any more she could end up with more pain and she can't handle that. She hardly speaks. I hear that vulnerable voice from time to time, but it's worse when I don't hear it at all. She speaks more frequently than she did a year ago, so that's good, but with recent circumstances I don't tend to have much time to think about any mental improvement she might have made.

At the time Nathan and I were together, mistaking and misunderstanding each other, Ryan was hurting Jessica, manipulating and menacing her.

I tell Zoe how Jessica is also battling cancer. This poor kind girl never gets a break. What did she do to deserve this? Nothing. That's the tragedy.

As I go on and on about Jessica's tragic life, Zoe kneels closer and closer to me. She wraps her arms around my neck and comforts me. I break down and cry.

CONFIDENTIAL

One day, I arrived at the Hub earlier than normal and Kim came out of her office to greet me in the hall. 'Morning, Ellis,' she said. 'Can I have a quick chat before you start?'

'Sure,' I said, wondering what I'd done wrong.

She took me into the small room where we'd had our first induction together. She looked very smiley.

'Ellis, I have some news I think you will be very happy with.'

'What is it?' I said.

'Well, it's actually two things. The first bit is that I've spoken to my manager, and it's a go-ahead for you to do that concert here.'

'That's brilliant!' I exclaimed. 'Nathan will be so pleased.' We'd asked Kim ages ago about this, and we'd kind of given up hope.

'What's the band called again?'

'Squeaky Pop Rockers.' I laughed.

'That's a mouthful!' said Kim.

'And what's the other thing?'

'The other thing is that there may be a chance that I can get you a paid work placement here at the Hub.'

'Oh. That's great, thank you.'

'Yes, well... it's not confirmed just yet so I would try to keep it to yourself, but I just wanted you to know that I am doing my very best to get this for you. I think you truly deserve it. You've worked above and beyond with so many of the service users, and they all talk very highly about you when you're not here.'

I was taken aback. 'Thanks, Kim! Made my day, you have.'

She smiled back.

Then I thought of something. 'But what about Nathan? I mean, he's been volunteering here longer than me. Is he also going to get paid work here?'

Kim's smile disappeared. 'Ellis, although Nathan has been very good to us, he hasn't come in as much as you have, which is why I feel that if I do get funding to take on another official staff member, I'd prefer it to be you. You come in almost every day of the week, and you stay most of the hours. Nathan just pops in on the odd occasion.'

'I have my off days as well,' I pointed out.

Kim sighed. 'You always inform me in advance. Nathan never really tells us when he's in or out. So, I have decided, if, cross fingers, this all works out, I will be choosing you and I hope you say yes.'

'If I didn't, would you give the job to Nathan?' I asked. I genuinely wanted to know.

Kim looked as though she was unsure how to phrase

what she was going to say. 'Not exactly, Ellis. You see, I don't know if you know this and it's a bit confidential, so I hope you don't mind me saying it.'

'I am not sure you should if it's confidential, Kim,' I said quickly.

'Well, it's not as such. Look, Nathan was a service user here before he was a volunteer. So, I don't think his mental health would be able to take the stress of working as an actual staff member. It's a lot of work and commitment when you are officially signed to work here. Poor Nathan, I don't think he'd be up for it.'

'But you don't know that,' I said. 'Nathan… I spend a lot of time with him. He has told me about his past, but he's a lot better now. Maybe if you speak to him, he might have a different perspective on it. He might be ready.'

'Sorry, Ellis,' Kim said. 'I won't be taking Nathan on. He's a lovely lad, but I don't want him to get worse again. I will let you know when it's confirmed, and if you are happy to sign up, I would love you to work with us.'

'Well… thanks,' I said, still not sure I felt entirely comfortable with the idea. But there was no point thinking about that now. I could always decline it later if I had to.

'Ellis?' she said to me as I was on my way out.

'Yeah?' I said.

'Look after him. I know he's a bit older than you, but he's very vulnerable. He may not show it most of the time, but I know he still needs the support.'

'Don't worry, Kim, I am there for him.'

'You're a lovely boy, Ellis.' She smiled.

STRICTLY

When I went into the office, Taz was in the kitchen making herself a cup of tea.

'Hello, Ellis,' she said.

'Hey, Tazzy,' I said.

'I watched *Strictly Come Dancing* last weekend.'

'It was good, wasn't it?' I said. I can never get enough of *Strictly*.

She nodded. 'That Aljaž Škorjanec is sexy.' She giggled.

'Aye, you're right there. He's good as well, isn't he?' I said.

'My favourite one ever was Harry Judd from a couple of years ago,' said Taz.

I nodded. I knew what she meant. 'That quickstep he did was incredible; the rhythm of the routine went beautifully with the song.'

'"Don't Get Me Wrong" by The Pretenders?'

'That's right, Taz.'

'My mam loves them. My dad said he fancies Chrissy Hines.'

'She's great, love her Christmas song too,' I said.

'Can I dance with you if they play it at the Christmas party?'

'Yeah, sure, why not? But I have to warn you, I am no Harry Judd.'

'That's okay. I'm like Aliona, so I can lead the way.'

'Fair enough.' I smiled.

STUPID

When I left the Hub at the end of the day, I gave Nathan a ring. Again, he hadn't been at the Hub that day, which hadn't especially helped when I was defending him to Kim.

'Hey, Nathan, you alright?' I asked.

'Oh, hey, Ellis! Yeah. Sorry I didn't come in. I am just so tired.'

'That's okay, you still like me to come over tomorrow?'

'Of course. Do some work?'

'Yes!'

'Sounds great.'

'Oh, and Nathan?'

'Aye?'

'Kim's finally given us an answer. We can use the Hub for our first show!'

'Great! Nice one, funny man.'

I wanted to tell Nathan about the other possible good news, that I could be getting a paid job at the Hub, but I knew that it wasn't a good idea.

'Oh, Ellis?' said Nathan.

'Yes?'

'If we finish in time, I thought we could watch some more *X-Files*?'

'Yes, that would be great,' I said. This meant we could snuggle on the sofa. We'd done that before; it was lovely.

When I finished talking to Nathan, I went to find Joel. I knew where he'd be – the benches near the arcade. He'd never had the best taste in chill-out spots.

I sat next to him and he gave me one of his chips from the cone he was eating out of. 'Sorry about the other week, mate,' he said.

'It's fine, Joel, honestly.'

Then suddenly I broke down and cried.

'Mate, what's the matter?' said Joel, looking a bit scared.

'I don't know. Joel, I am confused. I thought most of my life I was into girls, that I was going to marry the woman of my dreams. Now, I am into a boy. His name is Nathan. What if now I want to spend the rest of my life with him? I still find girls attractive. I just find boys attractive too, and I didn't realise it before. I don't feel bisexual. I just don't know. I need to know, don't I? I need to understand myself, my identity, my purpose. But how can I when I don't understand what I'm after and who I am? Who am I?'

Joel shrugged. 'You're Ellis.'

'Yes, I knew that much,' I said as I wiped the tears away from my eyes.

'No, I mean, you're Ellis. Gay, straight, bi… you're

just Ellis, and there's nothing wrong with that. You like boy bands, science-fiction, reading, music, and you find both sexes sexy. You fell in love with a girl, and now you're falling for a boy. Does it matter? As long as you're happy, mate.'

I couldn't believe it. This was the best thing to ever come out of Joel's mouth. I went in to hug him, as I couldn't believe how caring his words were.

'Hold on, mate, just to clarify, I am not gay,' he said, sounding alarmed.

I moved away and looked at him. I laughed and just said, 'I know you're not, you stupid twat. You're Joel. My stupid but best friend, Joel.'

JOEL

Joel stopped keeping in touch, which is a shame, because I had no issue with anything. Though, I will never tell him about the time me and Zoe slept together – I think that would drive him crazy. But there was nowt wrong with what we did. I liked Zoe, and it was after they broke up, and you know, we lived together, and we had drunk a bit too much beer. After that, I went through a bad patch. I went clubbing, and I started getting drunk and bringing hot girls home. A lot them were university students, but some were women my age or a lot older. It was just meaningless sex because I was completely lonely, and sex is good to forget about all your problems, but only in the time you're doing it. After that I was back feeling shit, so eventually I stopped. I started to feel guilty.

I still have the urge for sex, but I don't want to get closer emotionally with anyone. I don't want the risk of falling in love again. Sex and love, they're not the same thing. They go together well, but they can also be seen as separate things. I

JOEL

think a lot of people forget that, which is why they struggle to remain happy.

I never got with a guy after Nathan. I just had one-night stands with girls. I would watch Netflix and perv over Jude Law in some romantic film, watch Jason Merrells in my Lark Rise to Candleford *DVDs or wank over that social media star Cameron Dallas. But that's as far as I went.*

I only want to be with Nathan. He's the one that I truly love. To me, he was the soulmate, the life partner that everyone always says you should search for. Well, I didn't need to. He found me. I am grateful he did. Although it was short-term, we had to have found each other. We were meant to be together.

Now I am older, and I have been with more than one person and more than one gender, I realise that Nathan was the only person I actually fell in love with. I knew him only just under two years, but it was clear that he was the only one I truly felt right with. I miss him, I always will.

CARROT

The Christmas meal came so quickly; I couldn't believe it. I arrived at the Hub in the morning and saw the service users dressed in their Christmas jumpers. Taz was singing 'Do They Know It's Christmas?'. Her favourite song, she said to me. I told her I thought it had a nice tune, but I agreed with what Alice from *Vicar of Dibley* said about that song. I told her my favourite Christmas songs of all time were 'Don't Let the Bells End' by the Darkness, 'Fairytale of New York' by the Pogues and Wham!'s 'Last Christmas'.

'Oh, I love George Michael,' she said, and started singing his song instead.

I went around to greet the other service users. They all seemed in the Christmas cheer and mostly everything went smoothly, except for when I laughed at Malcolm's jumper. I had presumed that he realised that the snowman had the carrot missing from his nose and had it placed where his penis should be instead, but apparently not.

CARROT

I felt bad after I told him. He went all red and pulled it off straight away. Luckily, underneath he had an amazing shirt with tiny Christmas trees on it.

'Don't worry, Mal, have you got the receipt?' I said. 'I am sure they will give you your money back or swap it with another one.'

He nodded. 'Yes, you're probably right,' he said. 'I just wish I knew; I was looking forward to wearing that at the meal. But I don't think it's very appropriate.'

'Is your wife coming?' I asked.

'She is.'

'I look forward to meeting her.' I smiled.

Clive came up to me and told me all the latest bus times. He also told me that he knew all the Christmas number ones since 1952 and demonstrated this. His mind was incredible.

Sonia sat in the corner with a cup of tea in her hand. She was sat close to Rick. They were a couple now, apparently. I was so happy for them; they were really sweet together. It didn't mean Sonia stopped shouting at him whenever he came out with anything she felt was remotely stupid or sexist, which was a lot. I asked them if they would be together for Christmas. They told me they would, and we talked about the Christmas shows that were coming up that year. Sonia told me she would be watching all the soaps, and I told her I couldn't do that. Nathan had got me into *Hollyoaks*, but I couldn't watch soaps on Christmas Day itself. No way. They just shout and shout; it's not the time of year to be watching that. I told them I was looking forward to the *Doctor Who* Christmas special, and then I got caught up in discussing the fiftieth anniversary with Ben and Rick, which had been broadcast that year.

Time passed. I went around and chatted to everyone else. Nathan was giving out cups of tea. Once everyone was there, Kim came into the main room. She was wearing a knitted jumper with a gold star in the middle.

'The buses will arrive soon!' She beamed. 'To take us to our destination!' She seemed in the Christmas spirit, but that wasn't saying much.

FAGGOT

The buses took us slightly out of Harrogate to a pub restaurant on the outskirts. Even though Kim had booked it in January, she still didn't seem to have been able to find anywhere closer. All the way there we sang Christmas songs. It was warm on the bus, but once I stepped off the cold hit me. The view was lovely. Fields in white, with a sky of mist, floating across.

Once inside the restaurant I was supporting a young woman with Down's Syndrome called Lindsey. She didn't come to the Hub very often. She liked One Direction as well and had been to their concerts. She would tease me by showing me pictures of when she met them at a meet and greet once. She had her arms around Zayn, who she said was her favourite. I told her mine was Louis.

We sat at a table, next to Ben and his mother (who had arrived on her own; she told me that she'd done the shopping between dropping Ben off and coming here) and opposite us were Malcolm and his wife Clare. Clare had a perm and wore a very pretty and elegant dress. It was silver and radiant.

'Malcolm has told me you helped get his work sold at some shops?' said Clare.

'That's right. He has huge talent.'

'He does. And so do you, I've heard?'

'No, not really.'

'Malcolm says you sing well, and you are really caring.'

'I'm very flattered, but no, I can't sing. And caring… everyone should.'

'But not everyone does.' She shrugged.

'Malcolm told me you write poetry?' I said.

'Yeah, she does write some lovely poetry,' Malcolm added.

'I will have to read some sometime.' I smiled.

She nodded. 'I have a book I made once. I will get Malcolm to bring it in for you.'

'Thanks,' I said. 'I would like that very much.'

We pulled crackers as we waited for our food and read out the jokes that were inside.

'"What bees make milk?"' I read. '"Boo-bees."'

Ben howled with laughter. Malcolm and his wife laughed gently, and so did Lindsey. Ben's mother, on the other hand, looked mortified, but soon came round to seeing the funny side. 'Well, I suppose it is amusing, but isn't that a bit rude for Christmas? she said. (I privately thanked the Lord that Sonia wasn't in earshot.)

'What does yours say, Patricia?' I asked her.

'Mine says, "What's brown, steaming and comes out of Cowes? The Isle of Wight ferry."'

'I don't get it,' said Ben.

His mother sighed. 'Whatever happened to good old-fashioned jokes like, "When is a door not a door? When it's a jar!"?'

Soon our starters arrived – tom-tom soup. Then for mains we had turkey, with roast potatoes and veg. Then for dessert I had a mince pie and cup of tea. It was all yummy and filling; I would easily have gone there again – although so far, I never have done.

When everyone had finished their meals, it was time to dance and sing. There was a DJ in the corner of the room and Ben was the first one up.

'Oh, my goodness!' His mother laughed. 'Don't go complaining about indigestion now, will you?' she shouted over to him.

Lottie was up next, then Sonia, then Rick, and shortly afterwards everyone was up, apart from Morgan, Jane and Polly, who just stayed at the table moaning at each other. I really don't get why they were in this job.

Then 'Fairytale of New York' came on. I sang and swayed to this one.

Taz was laughing at me. 'Ellis!' She giggled.

'What's he like?' said Ben, who was also nearby.

When I got to the bit where Kirsty MacColl calls Shane McGowan a faggot, I looked over at Nathan and blushed, wondering if he'd be offended. He didn't seem bothered, though.

Afterwards I sat down for a rest, and Nathan came to sit next to me. 'You got the moves, haven't you?' he teased.

'I love that song. Sorry about the offensive language in it.'

'I beg your parsnips?'

'Faggot. It's not nice, is it? You're gay.'

Nathan laughed. 'I don't think anyone with any sense is bothered by that line. It just means "lazy" in context. You're gay these days, does it offend you?'

I thought about it. 'No, not really.'

'And it shouldn't. It's just the PC brigade getting offended on our behalf.'

The music played around us, and I stared into Nathan's hypnotising eyes. He looked stunning, gorgeous. I wanted to kiss him, but I didn't. We were at work.

Eventually we got back up and danced again with the service users. We danced to 'Daydream Believer' by The Monkees and all sang at the top of our lungs.

My gaze kept going back to Nathan. I watched him dance and sing with everybody. He looked incredible. I wanted to be his boyfriend. Why couldn't I be? We'd had sex and we always hung out with each other. I thought that perhaps I might tell him next time we were alone. Maybe he'd be alright with it by now. Then I remembered the other thing I had to tell him, and my optimism faded.

PRESENT

When I headed to the toilet, I bumped into Rick in the hallway. He looked downbeat.

'What's wrong?' I asked.

'It's Sonia, I upset her. I said something sexist apparently.'

'Where is she?'

'In the main room, sat at the table.'

I thought of the present I had brought with me, wrapped up in my rucksack, that I'd left in the cloakroom. I was going to give it to her, a present from me. But after a little consideration, I decided it'd be best if Rick handed it to her. That present would surely make up for all his stupid remarks.

'Hold on,' I said. 'Wait here.'

I ran ahead to get the present from my rucksack and ran back quickly to Rick. 'Here,' I said.

'What's that?' he said.

'It's a beautiful handbag that you're going to give to

Sonia, and she will open it and truly fall in love with you.'

'Ellis, I can't. If you bought it, you should give it to her.'

I shook my head. 'Nonsense. Please, don't think anything of it. I want you to give it to her. You love her, and this will bring you both such happiness.'

'Cheers, mate.' He beamed, and he wheeled off into the main room with the present resting on his knees.

I followed in shortly afterwards, and I looked over at Sonia. She had already unwrapped the gift. She was beaming from head to toe, and she looked in awe at the present, but not as much awe as when she looked into Rick's eyes. She hugged him and kissed him, and I smiled to myself and went to sit down at my table, as I watched the rest of the room dance.

MISTLETOE

That night, Nathan and I walked through town together. We walked past all the shops with Christmas decorations in the windows. The lights across the main part of town were glinting above our heads. Nathan must have finally been feeling the cold. He was looking all snug in his Christmas jumper and scarf.

I felt something rest gently on my nose. It was white and magical. I reached out my hand and then looked up. It was starting to snow. The sky was dark, and the backdrop looked like the best Christmas card that you would ever receive.

I looked at Nathan and he smiled at me. He got a spray of mistletoe out from his pocket and raised it above our heads.

'What are you doing?' I said. 'I thought you didn't like people seeing you kiss me and hold my hand.'

'I've decided I don't care anymore,' he said. He

blushed. 'Plus, the fact I am falling for you. I want to kiss you, and I don't care who knows it.'

I smiled. I could see the reflection of my eyes in his, and they grew larger as I went in to kiss him. As we kissed, I felt a warm feeling inside my belly, and it wasn't the food from the meal.

If Nathan was also falling for me, did that mean I could tell him my good news about getting the job without him getting mad? Would he be happy for me? I hoped so. I couldn't say no to that job; surely, he would understand that?

I decided to stop thinking about it for now. Maybe I'd tell him when we put together our plans for our first concert at the Hub. But for now, I decided to enjoy the moment. The sweet kiss of Nathan.

VULNERABLE

I walk around the supermarket, helping Jessica with her shopping. She stares into space while I check through the shopping list that I helped her put together. I let her rest her hands on the trolley as I stand in front, moving in the direction we need to go. This is the first time we've done this. One of Jessica's therapists recommended it as a way of increasing her independence again, but so far I've been the one doing most of it.

We buy chicken wings and eggs, milk and cereal. We gather most of the vegetables that are on offer. Salad and cream. Some yoghurts, strawberry and coconut. That's her favourite dessert.

I look at her and smile, but she isn't watching me. I rest my head onto hers. Then I step back and look at her again. She almost smiles. That's enough. I move on.

As I'm looking for rice, Morgan appears at the opposite end. My heart speeds up, and I can feel my forehead begin to sweat. She hasn't seen me, and I don't want her to. I look around for an aisle we can duck into without too much trouble.

An elderly man close to her has dropped his stick. He tries to hold onto the packet that's in his hands, but it goes flying.

Morgan picks them both up and hands them back to the elderly gentleman. He smiles at her gratefully, and she smiles back, before heading off in a different direction.

It's weird to see Morgan in that situation. In that moment, she cared for someone. She actually stopped what she was doing to help a stranger. If only she'd done that with the people she worked with. She was better than Jane and Polly, but that wasn't saying much. I won't forget all the shit that those three put Lottie through. The way they treated the service users as well. Not good at all. This doesn't change any of that. I should have spoken out back then; I should have made more of a stand. So, what does that make me? Perhaps I am no better than they are. I know I didn't treat the service users badly, but if I didn't stick up for them over the people that did treat them badly, I can't really complain. All those vulnerable voices, and what did I do about it? Nothing.

I was caught up with one particular vulnerable voice. The one that I loved. I tried to be there for him and do everything I could to make him happy, but it wasn't good enough.

CHICKEN

This was the day I remembered most. It was because the few days before were the best and then it all changed in a second. The previous couple of days I was going regularly to the Hub, and then back home to chill with Mam and Dad. We played board games after tea most nights, and in between I found time to meet up with Nathan. We did all the usual stuff we did together, and we even kissed and had sex a few more times.

I was on my way to see him, at his uncle's house. I had just had a great day at the Hub, and I'd had a chat with Kim going through all the details about the concert. It was really starting to feel real. I was in good spirits, and at that moment I wasn't even thinking about Nathan finding out.

I didn't tell him straight away. When I arrived, he was cooking. He let me in, and I joined him in the back of the kitchen as he carried on making his food.

'How was your day?' he said.

'Good.'

'Just good?'

'I guess.'

He looked back at the food which was frying in the wok. 'I am making us a chicken stir-fry,' he said.

'Oh, that sounds lovely,' I said. 'Thanks, Nathan. You're too good to me.'

'It's alright, I enjoy it. It isn't a chore.'

'I will have to cook something for you in the future.'

'You can cook?'

'Yes. I've got a list of recipes that I wrote down when I used to watch *Big Cook, Little Cook*.'

Nathan turned to look at me again. He laughed. 'Funny man. If you hadn't earned that title before, you certainly have now.'

'They made some good stuff,' I said.

'I'm sure they did. Hey, why don't we go upstairs? I have something to show you.'

'But what about the food?'

'It can cook itself for now. I will be down to check it in a bit.'

He led us up to the bedroom and showed me what was on the screen. It was an email from a different band to the one we had booked, asking us to get them a show. Our social media must have been working, and our name was getting out there. It meant we could start organising our second show as well as our first.

'Oh, that's great!' I said. 'It's all coming together.'

'Yes, I guess so! After food we can start making more plans. Try and get it all confirmed.' He smiled at me. 'Ellis, I'm so glad you came to volunteer at the Hub.'

I nodded. Then I looked guiltily into Nathan's eyes. 'What is it, Ellis?' he said.

I panicked. He could sense I was thinking something I wasn't happy about. 'Kim told me some other news the other day,' I said eventually. Actually, it was several months ago, but I didn't want him knowing how long I'd been sitting on this.

'Right?'

'I hope you will be happy with what I am going to tell you.'

'Depends on what it is. You're not being kicked out, are you?'

'No,' I said slowly. 'Well, actually I've got two things to tell you.'

'Spit it out, Ellis.' He smiled.

'Okay. Well, the first is, if we are going to keep going with this, I need clarification. I need to know if I am your boyfriend now.'

'No,' he said. His straightforward, quick and easy answer made me feel like hell. I didn't realise it was going to hurt me so much. I felt like all my flesh had melted and my skin was floating like Casper the Friendly Ghost.

'Right,' I said. 'Why is that? I thought at Christmas you might change your mind.'

'Well, I haven't.' He sighed. 'Look, Ellis, we're good mates, and now and then we fool around. What's wrong with that?'

'Well, I thought we could have been something more. I was beginning to think you were falling for me. You know, like that kiss after the Christmas meal. Wasn't that love? You said it was.'

'No, Ellis. I probably drank a bit too much at the meal. It was just two mates having a bit of fun. Kissing, sex. It's just a laugh.'

'Well, not for me. I thought it was more than that. Something special. Am I just some big joke to you then? Funny man? Is that all I am?'

He looked intensely into my eyes. His head came close to mine. 'Ellis, you are special, and I do like you very much. I am just not wanting a relationship. Don't take it personally.'

'Well, I am.'

'Then don't.'

'Jessica did this to me, you know.' Nathan sighed. I continued speaking. 'I thought she loved me, then she just broke up with me. The day I left school; it was almost my eighteenth birthday. Everything should have been grand, but she made it turn to shit. You see, I loved her, and she didn't love me. I thought she did, but she told me that we weren't right, that there was someone else out there for me. At first, I thought she was crazy, but after enough time thinking about it, I accepted it. Then when you came along, and I started to realise you liked me and I liked you, I thought you were the right one for me. You led me on, Nathan. I knew you fancied me from day one.'

'No, you didn't.'

'Okay, from day two.'

'More like day twenty-six. And anyway, you're the one that stripped for me.'

'You didn't object. And before that, you kept saying

how great and handsome I was. Don't make this out to be my fault.'

'It's no one's fault, mate. Anyway, what's the other thing you wanted to talk to me about?'

The moment I'd been dreading had arrived. But after all, he had hurt me, so it kind of made it easier in the end to tell him. 'I got a job,' I said to him, sounding smug.

'What, a paid one at last?'

'Yes.'

'Nice one, funny man. Where at?'

'The Hub.'

There was a pause. I watched Nathan's eyes as they tried to retain the last thing I said.

CONGRATULATIONS

'You are getting paid to work at the Hub?' he said.

I nodded. 'Nothing's signed yet, but Kim said it's basically mine as soon as I want it.'

'Well, congratulations,' he said unenthusiastically. 'I don't suppose they have a position for me?'

I shook my head. 'They only had one position and they went for me.'

Looking back, I realise I said that with no emotion, but Nathan had upset me by not wanting to be my boyfriend and still leading me on. I wanted someone to love me, but I kept finding people that just used me. It wasn't fair.

I looked at Nathan. He looked angry, even though all he was doing was standing still and staring into space.

'So, what do you want to do now?' I said at last.

He screamed and I stepped back.

'Nathan, I'm sorry. I have to take the job. I hope you understand.'

CONGRATULATIONS

'Congratulations!' he screamed. He started to hit his head. I grabbed his hands, trying to pull them away.

'Get off me!' he shrieked, and I fell towards the wall. I felt my head hit against it. 'Get away, Ellis! Piss off!'

'Nathan, you don't mean—'

'I do, fuck off!'

I stood up slowly, rubbing my head. I could see him crying.

'Nathan, it's alright, mate. You will get a job—'

'I don't want any fucking job! I worked my arse off there before you came along. But they all loved you more.'

'That's not true!'

'Yes, it is! It is fucking true! You go in every day, and they all love your funny ways, but I've done so much more there, and this is how they repay me. It's not fucking fair.'

'I don't know what to say.'

'Just fuck off, Ellis.'

'Nathan, I don't want this to come between us.'

'Well, there isn't an us, is there? I don't want to be with you. I don't love you. Never have, never will.'

'Fuck you!' I shouted. I had completely given up on feeling sorry for him. He was crushing my heart.

'Get out!' he said. 'Fuck the promotion company, fuck our friendship. Bye, Ellis.'

He started to bite his hands. I grabbed hold of them and he tried to fight me off. I ended up wrestling him to the ground. 'Get off!' he screamed.

'I can't let you hurt yourself like that!' I screamed back.

Suddenly the hairs inside my nostrils were twitching

and then I started to cough. I could smell strong smoke wafting into the room.

'Can you smell that?'

'Smell what? Who cares, get out!'

The smoke started to trail into the room. Even though for some reason Nathan couldn't smell it, he must have seen the dark, eerie cloud that had floated in and was obscuring the walls. The smell got stronger, and at last Nathan smelt it as his hand touched his nose.

'Nathan, shit, it's smoke! I think it must be coming from the cooking.'

Nathan's eyes bulged as he pushed me out of the way. He ran out of the room and down the stairs, with me in hot pursuit. 'Shit, shit, shit!' he spluttered, but he was coughing heavily in between. There was smoke pouring out of the kitchen.

'Nathan, get out! Come on.'

He was ignoring me, as he tried to get towards the kitchen to turn it off. I don't know why, as the damage was done. I grabbed his arm to try and pull him out of the front door. But he was resisting and making it really hard. He was a lot stronger than I was. He got away from me, and he started to scream and hit against the cupboards.

'Why does everything end up going wrong?' he screamed.

I looked in and my heart sank. The oven was going up in flames.

'Nathan, please try to calm down,' I shouted. 'We've got to get out of here, now!'

Nathan wasn't thinking straight. He grabbed a nearby

glass and whacked it against his leg. The glass smashed. Most of it cut Nathan's hands and then they started to bleed.

CHIMNEY

With Nathan's injured leg, it took all my strength to get him out of the house.

He was coughing and looked like he was about to faint. I dragged him away from the house and rested him on some gravel. There was no one about; the house was in the middle of nowhere. I checked my phone and luckily, I could get a signal. I rang 999 and asked for an ambulance and the fire brigade to come straight away.

Then I bent down and hugged Nathan closely to my chest. 'It's all going to be okay, Nathan,' I said. 'You're going to be fine.'

I started to cry. My tears falling from my eyes and on to his face. He looked like he had fallen into a chimney.

I'd been so focussed on getting him out of the house I hadn't really noticed until that point the burns he'd sustained. I'd always thought burns were red, or maybe black, but Nathan's were weirdly pale. I was relieved I'd got him out before it could do any more damage, but it looked really bad.

'Nathan, please say something,' I said.

His eyes were closed. I placed my hand gently to his chest. I could feel his heart pumping, so I knew he was alive. But he looked dead, and this made me cry even more. I waited, holding him close until eventually the ambulance came.

When the firefighters arrived, they shot right past us to get the fire down in the house. I hadn't even thought about the house. I'd forgotten all about it. The flame that mattered most was mine and Nathan's. He'd said he didn't love me, but he must have done. He was just scared to take responsibility.

'Help him!' I screamed, and two of the paramedics came to pick him up and put him in the ambulance.

'Will he be alright?' I said, as someone put a blanket over me. I shrugged it off. 'I don't need a blanket, just tell me if he's going to be alright?'

'We are going to need you to calm down,' said one of the paramedics. It was a woman in her fifties and I could tell she was doing her best to be calm and caring, but it didn't matter. I have seen her before. She works with my mam, so I've seen her about. She didn't recognise me though. She kept repeating what she was saying, but I struggled, just wanting to get inside so I could place my arms around Nathan. I needed to be with him. Her voice started to rise. She was doing her job, and it annoyed me. I know it shouldn't have done and that she was only trying to help, but I was lost in panic. I started to scream.

'Please can you calm down?' she said. 'Everything is being taken care of. You've just got to stay calm.'

'How can I?' I said. 'He's hurt, and it's all my fault.'

I carried on crying. I started to lose my balance. Another paramedic came up to me. Another woman, closer to my age. Then everything became a blur.

NATHAN

Next minute, I woke up in the hospital bed. I opened my eyes. Mam and Dad were there, looking down at me.

'Where am I?'

'Oh, Ellis!' said Mam. She grabbed me and hugged me. When she stepped away, I noticed she was sobbing.

'What's going on?' I asked.

'You were caught in a fire,' said Dad. He was also sobbing. I'd never seen him like that before. 'Thought we were going to lose you,' he sobbed. 'What happened, Ellis?'

Mam gave me another hug.

It took me a while to remember everything, but soon it all came back to me.

'Nathan!' I shouted. 'Is he alright?'

UMBRELLA

Life is just existence, and people who struggle with that think. They constantly think. That's what Nathan told me once. Probably in our breaks between skateboarding or working towards our promotion company. No... of course it was none of those times, as the only time he really told me the innermost emotions that were caged inside his beating heart was after sex. I didn't get what he meant at first, but I do now. He said that the people who really think are the ones that greet pain in ways most folk would never understand. Again, he lost me at that point. But my expression must have showed, as he would always laugh and then simplify his meaning. I think the basic principles of what he was saying are basically what I'd told him myself once – that he thought about everything in too much detail, and that was too much for him to handle. Love, politics, art, purpose – he would analyse the world with more care than he should.

He said that's why he liked me. It was because I didn't

think. When he first said that I wanted to hit him hard with the pillow that was resting behind my head, but instead I gazed into his eyes and he laughed. Again, I must have shown how I felt all across my damn face. He apologised, as he knew how it must have sounded, but he tried to explain what he had actually meant, and I didn't mind at all. It was the kindest thing that anyone had said to me my entire life. He said, 'Funny man, you're the best thing I have ever come across, because you are genuine. You are kind not because you have to be, but because you just are.'

'So are you,' I said to him.

He just shook his head and said that wasn't true.

'Yes, it is,' I said. 'You just told me that the reason you like me is because I am honest, so let me be honest with you now. Nathan, you are just as kind as me. The only problem is you have an illness that affects your personality. You have the common cold for mentality. There is a dark cloud that hides your true self, that's all. You will be okay because dark clouds don't last forever. They come and go.'

'And how do I ignore these metaphorical clouds?' he asked.

I paused, and eventually said, 'Take an umbrella wherever you go?'

He looked at me. He knew I was being serious, but he couldn't help himself. He burst out with laughter.

Then he swooped in and kissed me. His hands grabbed my waist and he slipped himself between my thighs and started to thrust.

PATIENT

The doctors wouldn't let me out to begin with. I eventually calmed down, but I couldn't help the tears dripping down my cheeks.

Mam and Dad sat with me. They didn't talk. Mam just threw her arms around me and comforted me. I pushed her away, starting to freak out again. 'I need to see him,' I said.

'Ellis, please,' said Mam. 'The doctor isn't going to let you if you behave like this.'

'Why not? I'm not ill. I fainted, that's all. I need to go and find him.'

'He's alright,' said Dad.

'How do you know?' I asked.

'Because the doctor has told us.'

I started to calm down again. This time I forced myself to, as I knew that the more I acted this way, the longer it would be before I could see Nathan.

I told Mam I was sorry and looked at her with a smile.

'It's just a shock,' I said. 'It all happened so fast.'

'I know,' said Mam. 'I came straight up as soon as Nina said.'

Of course, Mam worked here. I hadn't taken in that she was still in her work uniform. Nina was her friend who she worked alongside in her department. Not a nurse, but the person who types up all the files on each patient who comes into the hospital. She must have seen my name come through and told Mam straight away.

'I phoned Dad, and he came as quickly as he could.'

'Yes, but if I was to know you was going to not wake up until this point, then perhaps I would have finished the car I was repairing, had some scampi and chips, and then come down to see to you.'

I closed my eyes and waited for my mam to say, 'Barry!' But when I opened them, she was just staring at me, pressing tightly into the palm of my hand.

HEAT

The next day I was completely fine, so fine that Dr Martin let me leave my bed. My parents stayed with me through the night, and when I was given the go-ahead to leave, Dad went back to his garage and Mam went back downstairs to her department.

I sat in the waiting room, waiting until I was allowed to visit Nathan. It's bizarre, because I knew he had more damage than me, but apparently, he regained consciousness quicker than I did.

I was reading *Heat* magazine while I waited. I found out that Cheryl Cole was having her nails done, Justin Bieber had spat in someone's face and that Paris Hilton's boobs were needing to be re-sized. Honestly, who reads this rubbish?

I'm not sure when I noticed the woman sitting opposite me, but she had the same auburn hair as Nathan's. Her face reminded me of his a lot, but it had more weight to it. Her body was not as slim and fine-tuned. She was large but her eyes shone with amiability, with drops of melancholy spiralling in her pupils.

She caught my eye, like a wild animal lost in the desert, facing off against a predator. 'Are you Ellis?' she said. I nodded. 'You're the boy who saved him.'

'I did?'

She nodded. 'So he tells me.'

'Who, Nathan?'

She nodded again. 'That's right.'

'Oh. Okay, that's good. I was worried it was my fault we were in this mess.'

'It is.' I looked at her, not understanding. 'He told me you did it: you caused the fire. But it was an accident. In the end, you saved him. You got him out the house and you called 999. I don't think he would still be alive if it wasn't for you.'

Then she leapt at me, quicker than I thought any woman of that size could, and squeezed me tightly. I tried to push her back in case she suffocated me. Luckily, she moved back, and I gasped for air.

'Sorry, love,' she said. 'Don't know my own strength.' She then sat back down, but this time by the side of me. 'Thank you. I don't know how much you know about what you have done. But Nathan has been a lot happier since you came into his life. He didn't tell me much about you to start off with, but I saw a difference in him, and the only thing that's changed in his life since he's become like this is meeting you. He still has his off days, but the days before he knew you, trust me, he was a wreck. You get him, and he appreciates that. That's what I think. Not a lot of people do, including myself, but even the people I thought did get him, they don't the way you get him. I can hear his voice change, I can feel life in him, even if he just briefly mentions your name. I know.'

I looked at her and smiled. It was a genuine smile, because that's who I am, as Nathan told me himself. But I could sense my face going as red as the blood-coloured rug below us. Did Nathan really think I was the saviour? Had he already come to the conclusion to forgive me? Or had he lost his memory? If he hadn't, then I was surprised he remembered I saved him. If he remembered this, then perhaps he remembered the row. I was so nervous about seeing him now that when one of the nurses finally arrived, I insisted that his mam should go first, even though she'd said that I could.

What if he'd just said all the good stuff to his mam to stop her getting more upset than she must be already? Surely, when I went to see him, he would be there, not calling me 'Funny man' anymore, but 'sad man', 'evil man', 'treacherous man'. I don't know. But I had a sick feeling inside my belly that was giving me the idea that he wasn't going to be so humble when our eyes met.

INFECTIOUS

I was completely wrong. As soon as I entered Nathan's ward, his eyes danced in the stream of light that shot through the glass of his bedside window.

'Ellis!' he shouted, sounding excited.

'Hi, Nathan,' I said nervously. I was so pleased that he didn't seem annoyed or wanting to get rid of me.

I sat on the chair close to his bed. There was a nurse fiddling around with something, but she didn't pay me much attention. I quickly glanced over at his bedside table. There was just a half-empty glass of water on there, that made me feel half empty inside. I felt guilt, shame and everything that someone would in this situation. He didn't have a vase with bright yellow flowers in them, like I had done. Nana sent me them. She had a bad cold and couldn't come to see me in person. I also had a couple of get-well cards. One from Jessica, saying she hoped to visit me soon, and one from Joel. Nathan had nowt. At least his mam was there for him.

'Ellis, before you say anything else, I want you to hear me out.'

'Okay,' I said. If he wasn't speaking so softly and his eyes weren't so gracious, I may have jumped out the window and done a runner. Strangely, he didn't seem at all cross with me.

'Ellis, I am sorry.'

'What for?' I said.

'Everything.'

'But you've done nowt.'

'That's not entirely true.'

'It isn't?'

'No. I left the cooking on, if I am not mistaken. We had a row, but I should have been keeping an eye on the cooking. And anyway, about the row... from what I remember, I think it was because I told you I didn't love you.'

I shook my head slowly.

'Well, Ellis, no one can blame a man who falls in love.'

'I can't blame you for not loving me back.'

'I do love you, Ellis.'

'What?'

'I said I do love you, but it's not that simple. I can't be with you.'

'Why not?'

'It's complicated.'

'No, it's not,' I said. 'You just make it sound more complicated than it needs to be.'

'I do?'

'Yes,' I said. 'Nathan, remember that time you tried

to tell me how you struggle with life? It's just the same as with love. Love is existence, but you can't bring yourself to love even when you find it. You have always wanted this, I know you have, but you think too much. Thinking too much brings fear; it brings dilemmas. It brings misery, unless you write it into a book or a song. But you're not a character in a book or a song. You have a life that's real, so stop thinking and let your love float. I care about you, and I know you care about me, so let's just be together. Let's enjoy life together without thinking, and let's just have a laugh.'

He stared at me for a while, as if he weren't quite in the room, but he was and his eyes soon gleamed again. 'Okay, funny man. You're on.'

'You mean you will give it a go? Me and you?'

'Yes, because you're right. You're always right.'

'No, you are,' I said.

'Well, that's true, but you've used my philosophy and twisted it to make me see a bigger picture that I didn't realise was there. Life should be cherished as much as possible. I was scared of loving you, Ellis, but now I don't need to be scared, because love is the last thing you should be scared of. We don't know when our lives will end, so we must try to live it with happiness and not let our fears take over.'

I smiled at Nathan.

'Ellis,' he said.

'Yes?'

'It's going to be okay.'

'Isn't that the kind of daft line I would have said?'

'Yes, funny man, that's true. I guess it's infectious.'

'Oh, heck.' I chuckled.

'Ellis?'

'What is it, Nathan?'

'How is everyone back at the Hub?'

'I've not heard.'

'Okay, well… you know the band we booked? I want you to go ahead with it.'

'I will, but won't you be there as well?'

'No, we booked them for 12th March. I won't be out by then.'

'Oh, right,' I said in disappointment. 'We can always delay it until you're fit and ready.'

'It's okay, Ellis. You will be fine without me. I think you should still go ahead; it will help us move our business forward. If all goes well, when I get out of here, we can work towards the next show. I'm sure Lottie will help you out in the meantime.'

And on cue, there she was. Lottie. She came hurrying towards us, with a large envelope in her hand.

'Excuse me, madam, but only one visitor at a time,' said the nurse.

'It's okay,' I said. 'I was about to leave.' I got up from my seat.

Lottie gave me a big hug after she handed over the large envelope to Nathan.

'How are you, Ellis?' she said.

'I'm good.'

'Thank heavens for that. I spoke to your mother, lovely woman,' said Lottie. 'She told me you were now conscious, so I came as quickly as I could. That card there, it's signed by everyone back at the Hub. Sorry it took me so long to bring it; I wanted to make sure everyone you knew down the Hub had signed it. Of course, they are not all there, every day. But I got there in the end. Go on, open it.' She smiled.

Nathan did, and inside was a huge get-well card.

Lottie's eyes were filled with tears as he opened it and we all peered our heads over to look at what everyone wrote.

'Stupid boys, playing with fire,' she said while she was wiping her eyes and stepping away from Nathan's bed.

'We weren't playing with it,' I said. 'Just—'

'Silly boys, I'm just glad you're both alright.'

'I'll let you have some time with Nathan. I am going to go and get a coffee in the café area and something to eat. I am so hungry.'

'Okay, love, I'll meet you down there,' she said. 'Wait for me, will you? We need a good old catch-up.'

'Sure thing, Lottie.' I grinned. I gave one more look to Nathan, who gave me a wink and said, 'Take care, funny man.'

TEARDROP

I continued to work hard organising the event for 12th March. Nathan was still at the hospital, and I didn't want to let him down. Squeaky Pop Rockers were on their way to Harrogate. They had just done a show in Newcastle and were finishing their tour with us. The band members were in their mid-twenties and looked the bees' knees, and you could see their knees and all… I mean, they wore those jeans with the holes ripped through. Nathan would call it rock 'n' roll, but I just call it strange. They'd seemed like a bunch of lads when Nathan and I had communicated with them through email. They had a manager that they passed me on to, but he seemed useless. I ended up communicating with the lead singer on everything in the end. His name was Darren Milks. I told him that I loved how they blended multiple genres. He thanked me. Then I thought about the CD Nathan had given me, and how much I cherished it.

I was listening to that most of the time at that point,

but I still loved my One Direction, JLS and, whatever Nathan said, I thought McFly and Busted were really good and sounded just as rock 'n' roll as the band we'd booked for the Hub. The guys in Squeaky Pop Rockers had long hair, not a look I normally go for, but their faces were so pretty and made lumberjack shirts a thing.

Nathan was meant to open up for them, but of course he couldn't now. So instead, I'd asked Rick if he wanted to play some songs on his guitar. He was honoured when I asked him and said yes straight away.

I was walking around the room greeting everyone that had come to the concert. Jessica was by me the whole time. She'd come all the way up from Bath to support me. That was sweet of her. She'd dropped her posh totty accent, but she was still acting odd at times. At this point I think she was still with Ryan, so who knows what she was thinking about.

I thought to myself how there was still a part of me that loved that girl. She was so beautiful and a lot of fun. But she didn't love me in the end, and that was alright, because I had Nathan. Jessica was becoming more like a best mate. Sod Joel. Speaking of Joel, he was there as well. He'd brought Zoe. She was a nice girl. Strange, but nice. She was a fan of the band that I'd booked and told me that I was super dope to get them. I thought to myself that I didn't quite get why I was drugs for booking this band. She was smoking-hot too. *Nice one, Joel*, I thought. Hopefully, this girl would do good for him. She was zany like Joel – zany Zoe, I called her whenever I spoke about her to Jessica – but she had brains. Not that Jessica didn't, just that Zoe was studying Biological Sciences at the University of York. I mean, brains or what!

Ben ran up to us when we were huddled in our group. Jessica was holding on to a cup filled with squash and Joel had his arm around Zoe.

'Hi, I am Ben. I am Ellis's boss.'

'You're not my boss,' I corrected him.

'Ellis, don't chinwag to your boss like that,' said Zoe. (I immediately went off the girl.) 'My name is Zoe. It's totes amazeballs to meet you, Ben.' I didn't think Ben would understand that, but he didn't look confused.

'Let me introduce you to my mam,' he said, and off Zoe and Joel went to mix with the crowd.

'You should be proud of yourself, Ellis,' said Jessica. 'Getting a concert set up for your service users and the locals, and such a cool band, how did you manage that?'

I told her it just took a bit of persuading, and a lot of my savings.

She laughed. 'Honest?'

'That's me,' I said, thinking of Nathan.

Rick was getting his gear together. I rushed over to make sure he was alright. Lottie's husband Phillip was close by. He was helping with all the technical shit. He was so good at it.

'Oh God, you're not going to sing as well, are you?' said Sonia, who was standing close to the small stage which I'd created by putting a couple of Rostra together and attaching a ramp. She put her hand across her forehead.

'Oh, thanks for that,' said Rick. 'Great to have the support from your girlfriend like that.'

'You said you were going to just play your guitar, not sing as well.'

'I have a good voice.'

'Sure you do,' she said.

'I have had singing lessons, I'll have you know?'

I introduced Sonia to Jessica, and she said it was great to meet my girlfriend at last. I had to quickly correct her that Jessica and I were just friends. In fact, everyone we went around to chat to ended up thinking we were a couple, a lovely couple. I could sense Jessica was embarrassed. But she didn't say anything, I could just tell. I wasn't that bothered. I could have gone around spreading the word about me and Nathan, but I thought it was best to wait until he was out of hospital so we could tell everyone together.

In fact, why did we have to tell everyone? Holding hands as we walked would give enough indication. I remember when Nathan was uncomfortable with that before, but he wouldn't be now. I was sure of it.

We bumped into Taz, Lindsey, Maxi and Isabella. They were all dressed up like rock-star chicks. They had T-shirts with band names on, like The Ramones, The Rolling Stones – oh, and Lindsey and Taz had their One Direction tops on. I guess they weren't so rock 'n' roll, but they wore jeans, and they had holes in them and all.

When I introduced them to Jessica, they said that she was pretty and that she reminded them of Taylor Swift. It was Taz that pointed it out, but all their heads nodded after she stated it.

Shauna was there. She was eating the hot dogs and

cakes that Lottie was serving. She laughed after every bite. When she spotted me, she shouted my name as if I were one of the members of The Beatles. I waved discreetly, as I was embarrassed whenever she did this. Jessica smiled and said, 'So she must be Shauna – I remember you telling me about her.'

I introduced them to each other. Again, Shauna was another person to think Jessica and I were together. After several attempts to try and explain we weren't she then got distracted as she saw the band come through the door.

There was a loud cheer from some others after Shauna gave the game away. I quickly ran up to them, and when I spotted Darren Milks and introduced myself, I thanked him again for doing the show and told him where his band could put their equipment before they went on. I said that they could all wait in the meeting room or stay here. Whatever suited them best.

Jessica and I went back around to mingle with the crowd. We bumped into Clive, which surprised me as I was worried it may not have been his scene but was pleased he'd come. He wasn't usually someone to socialise in large groups, so it was great I had managed to get him out of that shell.

When he caught my eye, he came right up to me and told me what the council were planning with new bus routes which were apparently changing that April. Then he turned to Jessica, and after I introduced her to him, the first thing he said was, 'Do you like buses, Jessica?'

After chatting about buses, the trauma that Maggie

Thatcher had brought to the world and Eurovision songs, Clive left us to it as he went to help himself to a hot dog.

We saw Malcolm and Clare. They were standing in the corner. We went up to them, and Jessica went on and on about how beautiful Clare looked. She did look great. They both did. All the time, in fact. Always immaculately dressed. But Clare had really outdone herself tonight: her dress was shimmering and sparkling like an ice cave. They looked like they would have been better suited at an opera rather than a rock concert.

The room was filling up very quickly. We waved to Kathy and Ken, who had just arrived. He was wearing the hat that I'd got him.

Jessica told me afterwards that everyone seemed so nice. I told her they were, apart from the staff that didn't show that evening.

Lottie and Kim were there, of course, and they were incredibly supportive of the concert I managed to put together. But why Kim was wearing an ABBA-style costume and Lottie was dressed like Kate Bush I wasn't quite sure. I guess they were trying to be hip, but from the looks that Zoe was giving them, I don't think they were. They were dancing and yet the performances hadn't even begun. But soon enough, Rick started. The lights went dim.

When Rick started to sing, he did actually sound really good. He wasn't kidding about those singing lessons. Jessica and I went closer to the stage to watch, and I looked over at Sonia, who had a teardrop falling from her eye. She must have been amazed at how good he was. His guitar-playing was good as well, really good; just watching his hands fly up and down the fret board like that was hypnotising, and I mean it in a good way.

After a few songs, he said that he was about to play his last, which he dedicated to Sonia, and I could see her smiling and wiping the tears from her eyes.

'Give over, you soppy get,' she said. But I knew she was over the moon with how romantic Rick was being with her. She looked down at the floor, conscious that the now fully crowded room must have all been staring at her.

After Rick got off the stage and Squeaky Pop Rockers were getting set up for their performance, Jessica and I congratulated him and chatted to him about how he should continue with his music career.

'Thanks, mate,' he said to me. 'They are just cover songs.'

'I know,' I said, 'but that's what a lot of pubs around here are looking for. I'll certainly book you again.'

'Cheers, Ellis,' he said, and then he wheeled close to Sonia, who went in to give him a hug.

Jessica and I wandered around a bit, chatted to Ben's mother and someone else's mother, who turned out to be Taz's. They both congratulated me on my efforts.

Soon enough, the headline band was ready to play. The lights were dim again, but they had brought their own lighting system and smoke. It was like we had booked Bon Jovi. They put on one hell of a show. Pop punk mixed with indie and rock 'n' roll. Nathan would have loved it. I wished he had been here to witness this. My chest started to hurt. I tried to shake it off and convinced myself it was the vibrations from the amps that were making me feel that funny tingle inside my skin.

I looked around at all the happy faces. Everyone seemed to be enjoying themselves, and it was because of me. That made me feel good. Though I felt bad as I saw Ben's mother with huge pieces of cotton wool sticking out from her ears. I think it was a bit loud for her, but she seemed to be enjoying herself, nonetheless. She was bopping along, keeping an eye on Ben at the same time, who was thoroughly enjoying himself as he danced close to Maxi.

Joel was headbanging with Zoe. Taz was street-dancing, and everyone else was doing their own thing. I laughed when I watched Lottie and Kim. They looked a bit out of place, but I loved their enthusiasm. I think they were hoping for more of a disco vibe.

When the night was over, Jessica and I wandered back through the streets on our way home. I made sure to take her back to hers before I headed to mine. The sky was dark and dry, but the rain from earlier was on car bonnets and pavements and roads.

'Congratulations, Ellis,' she said as we reached her door.

'Thanks, Jessica,' I said. 'It was a great night.'

'It was, but that's not what I meant.' She kissed me on the cheek. 'Congratulations on getting with Nathan.' She then stepped back inside and smiled at me before she closed the door.

I just stood there for a while. Staring at her bright-red door that lit up this gloomy dark blue street. Was she some sort of fucking guru? I don't know how Jessica did this. I didn't tell her anything. But she knew. She always knew.

GHOST

After a night like that, it's inevitable that you'll feel low afterwards. I woke up feeling the worst. Not realising at the time that a whole lot of worse was heading my way. My whole body was bruised. Eventually, I got up. I looked at my clock and was surprised that no one had woken me up for breakfast.

I got out of bed and quickly put on some clothes that were lying on the floor the previous night. I thought, *I'll make breakfast and then shower and dress properly later on.*

I stumbled down the stairs, thinking, *Why on Earth did Mam not wake me?* But then, as I reached the bottom of the stairs, I could hear the clanking sounds of cutlery. Mam and Dad were home, and they were still having their breakfast. Was it the weekend and I had forgotten?

When I made it into the kitchen, Mam and Dad looked straight towards me. They both looked like they had seen a ghost.

'Is everything alright?' I said. 'Aren't you supposed to be in work?'

'Ellis, it's probably for the best you sit down,' said Dad shortly.

'Why, what's the matter? Why are you talking like that?'

Mam's cheeks looked pale and she moved her lips, but no voice was heard. Dad gave out a long and hard sigh. 'Your mother just got a call from Kim. It's not good news,' said Dad.

'What's not good news?'

'It's Nathan,' said Mam, finding her speech at last, but only just. 'Nathan passed away last night.'

I felt my whole body fill like a water tank. I could feel the water rising and wanting to burst out of all the holes of my body. My entire throat was welling up. I couldn't speak even if I'd wanted to. I lost all my train of thought. I now felt like the ghost floating through the air and this time I didn't feel like Casper. I think what I'm trying to describe was that I felt numb, completely and utterly numb.

Then I did something stupid. I screamed and punched the wall. I then ran back upstairs and wept into my pillow.

I was told afterwards, when I had calmed down enough to hear sense, that he died from a weak heart and the smoke from the flames. He had a very bad form of asthma. That whole scenario with the fire was too much for him.

MURDER

When I was little, all I did was listen to music. It was a way for me to escape the world in which I lived. I did this until I was nineteen, and then one day, someone that I loved died. I didn't care for music anymore. I know others find it a way to cope, and that's fine, but for me, I didn't. I came to learn that all life is about is trying to survive. I was lucky: I had kind parents that helped me get by, and I would survive by running away in my mind and listening to sounds that told me that fun could be had. Other people find other ways to survive. Now I just walk, and I observe. Observing means I can learn, and it means that life goes slower and I can just float through my thoughts and try to make sense of it all, but the truth is it doesn't make sense. Life is one big contradiction, and that's why we find it hard. Nathan said I didn't think, but that's because back then, I didn't have to. When you're young, you shouldn't, because there's plenty of time for that, and thinking too much brings too much pain and too much trouble. This is selfish of me, but I don't care.

I never recovered. How could I? That sort of thing will outlast all the happy memories. It stays with you like a curse. But I had to create a strategy to not let it destroy my entire life, which took a long time.

I stayed away from the Hub. I stopped staying in touch with everyone. I hardly spoke to Mam and Dad. Looking back, I was being stupid. I was pushing everyone away who was close to me and making myself feel more pain. But I deserved it.

Nathan didn't blame me in the end. If he'd never woken up, would people think I killed him? Would they really come to the conclusion that loveable boy next door Ellis was capable of murder? Well, hopefully not, because that is certainly not me. I couldn't even step on an ant. I even became vegetarian in time.

I loved Nathan, and now he's gone. Gone where exactly, I am unsure. I felt like someone had taken a big part of my soul and cut it in half.

I've realised recently that Sonia and Jessica are two women who got attacked by their partners. The difference is Sonia got with Rick, who is a wonderful guy who I know just wouldn't harm Sonia like that. I hope they're still together. Sonia came out on top in the end, but poor Jessica – it was the complete opposite. She had me, someone who would never do such a horrible and violent act, and yet she left me and found someone who was capable of such awful things. But I feel positive that one day Jessica will get better, find the right man (not that she needs one). I think love, if you can have it, is a wonderful thing. She will find someone who actually loves her, that she will love back, and she will be treated the way she totally deserves. I have faith in her. It will take her some time to get used to dating again, but when she's ready, I will be there with her all the way.

Occasionally when I walk around town or up to the Valley Gardens, on this bench where Nathan and I used to sit, I can feel the wind, and not like how I used to. When the wind is out, it's usually on days when I am thinking I need Nathan the most. The wind envelops me like a blanket, and I sense it's him. He's still out there somewhere, watching down and keeping me safe.

Truth is, the career I always wanted wasn't going to happen. I wanted to sing, but that dream boat sailed, and anyway, music reminded me too much of him. But that was fine. I've got into reading a lot more recently instead. Reading helps me relax. I read stories that take me away from my own problems. It also helps with my vocabulary.

The day after the McBusted concert with Jessica and Andy, I went to Nathan and told him I was sorry. I cried and kissed him. Well, not him, but the deck, which I buried in the Valley Gardens, where we used to skate and hang out. It sticks out of the ground, like a memorial, and it has his name engraved. It was one I made, for myself, so I could go and see him without the fear of bumping into his family or friends that go to visit his actual grave. I love him, and I always will. I will always blame myself as well. Because even though of course it wasn't intentional, I caused his death. It was my fault.

I sometimes think how he would look now if he were still alive. He probably wouldn't have changed much. He would be close to thirty now. I mean, I'm not far off that myself– scary. There's this American actor I keep seeing everywhere in films; he reminds me of him. They look the same. His name is Nick Robinson, and he was just as sexy as him. I told this to Zoe once, but I forgot to clarify I was on about Nick Robinson the actor, so for ages she thought I was on about Nick Robinson the political journalist who works at the BBC. She can be daft at times. No offence to that guy, but not my cup of tea, and certainly no resemblance to Nathan in looks.

When I was at that McBusted show, I remembered that if he knew I was there, he would have laughed at me, he would have called me Funny Man and said it was called a gig, not a show. I also remembered how he told me that when he was twelve, he would go to gigs right up till he was about nineteen and do things like mosh pit and crowd surf. I told him he was mental. What if he broke a leg?

He said going to gigs and singing to all his favourite bands was heaven to him. So was skateboarding with his mates, who he'd lost touch with by the time I knew him. I hope OPM were right, and that heaven is a halfpipe, because that would mean at least he is in heaven and having a good time. I wouldn't have even known who OPM were if it wasn't for him. He knew all these cool and quirky bands that I would have never heard of, and he got me into them. Before that all I listened to was One Direction and JLS.

FUNERAL

I was dreading this day, absolutely dreading it. But I went. We got the invite sent to us, don't know how. I never gave Nathan my address, but I guess his mam must have asked at the Hub and they had all my details.

The service was nice. I came on my own. Mam, Dad and Jessica had said they were happy to accompany me, but I told them I would be fine. None of them ever met him, which was strange because he was a big part of my life. I hadn't known him long, but I had known him enough to laugh, cry, get angry, have deep and meaningful conversations (and some silly ones), skate with each other, learn about better music, hug, have sex with, care for… and now to grieve.

I couldn't believe it. The last day I spoke to him, and he finally agreed to be my boyfriend, I walked home daydreaming of the life I thought we were going to have together. Grow old together. But no. I was almost twenty and I was already at the funeral of my other half. I'd known him less than two years and I felt I'd known him all my life.

Everyone was dressed in dark clothes with expressions of misery. At the front was a guy with a long beard. Was that Nathan's dad, I wondered? His mother couldn't bring herself to do her speech, so instead the vicar read it out. I should have built up the courage to have read out something or offered to read what she wanted to say. I could have told everyone how good Nathan was, and how he had so many skills and so many ambitions in life. How much love he had, even if he didn't quite know it. The stuff his mam had written astonished me. I could tell she loved him, but what the vicar was reading didn't sound like Nathan at all. She seemed nice, but why did she hardly know her own son?

I couldn't believe he died like this. Just because I got him worked up and made him forget that he was in the middle of cooking. I should have been the one in the coffin.

When the church music played out an old traditional song of sadness, I had a different song in my head play out. It was more fitting. It was track eleven from Nathan's mix CD. Secondhand Serenade – 'Your Call'. Then I broke down, my tears pouring out. I rested my head on my knees to hide myself away.

Once the service came to an end, I stayed put until the church was empty. Then I got up, intending to make my way to the pub where the after-gathering was taking place. I watched Nathan's parents shake the hand of the person that was just before me. When they left they looked up and saw me.

FUNERAL

'I am so sorry for your loss.'

'I bet you are,' said his father.

'I'm sorry,' I said, 'but I don't understand.'

'Bloody hell, are you simple or are you just playing games? Believe me, sonny, I don't like it when young pretty boys like you fuck me about.'

'I am not playing any games; I am serious with you. I don't understand.'

'What the fuck were you doing at my house without my permission?'

Then it clicked. 'You're Nathan's uncle?'

'Aye.'

'Then where's his dad?'

'None of your business,' said his uncle.

'Nathan and his dad never really got on,' said his mam.

'His son, his only son has died, and he can't be bothered to come and see him?'

'You've got a fucking cheek,' said his uncle. 'You're the fucker that burnt down my house and caused my nephew's death!'

'Murray, stop it, please,' said Nathan's mam. 'It wasn't Ellis's fault; in fact, it was Ellis that brought Nathan back to life.'

'What the fuck are you talking about, Moira?' said Murray.

'Since Nathan knew Ellis, I've seen he was happy again, motivated. He had dreams.'

'Well, all he will be doing now is dreaming.'

'Murray! Take that back.'

His uncle took a step back. I think he'd realised he'd

gone too far. 'Moira, I am sorry. I didn't mean anything of it.'

'Just go – go to the pub. I want to speak to Ellis in private.'

Murray didn't respond. He put his hands out in front of him as if trying to make peace between himself and Nathan's mother. He then gave me one nasty look before he walked out of the church.

'Ellis,' she said. 'Ignore Murray. He said Nathan could use his house when he was away, and if that meant Nathan wanted you there for company, then I see no issue with it. But there is one thing I want to say. Nathan's dad, he wasn't good to Nathan. He did love him. Nathan may have said differently, but I know deep down Frank loved his son. He was just the typical man who couldn't show his emotions, so instead he would just shout and shout. He wanted Nathan to be something he wasn't – that was the trouble. When Nathan was a little kid, he took him to all these football matches, but Nathan wasn't interested; he wanted to skate and go to rock concerts. Frank hated this, and would complain about Nathan's lifestyle, and Nathan never told us he was gay, but I knew he was. It was obvious in my eyes, but not so much for Frank, and Frank would constantly make horrible jokes and insults about gay people. I did tell him that I didn't approve, but he wouldn't stop. This obviously made Nathan turn completely against his father. Also, Nathan hated the fact his father called him weak, weak because he struggled with work and pressure. This is how his mental health got worse. I knew he had it since he was a child. We tried to give him a good life, but he was depressed and had had anxiety attacks since he was five years old. When Nathan got sectioned, his dad gave up on him. I was left to handle Nathan on my own, and you see, there was a year or so before he joined the Hub, where Nathan was in a really bad state. He would hit himself quite badly and he would scream and throw things around the room. And he would cry almost every night. His dad couldn't cope and left us. He divorced me and went on his own way. But Nathan, I saw the old Nathan again after you two met. He really liked you.'

I could feel myself welling up. I tried to speak and eventually I did. 'I know,' I said, 'in fact, he loved me. And can I just say, Nathan wasn't weak. Your husband Frank, he was weak. He was weak to walk out on you both just because he wouldn't try to support his own son.' Moira was nodding and weeping into her hands. I stopped talking and put my arms around her. 'It's okay – you did all you could, and he loved you too.'

She looked at me. 'He did?'

'He loved you so much.'

I kept my hands rested on her curved back and we slowly made our way out of the church and into the pouring rain.

HAPPY

At the pub I saw Lottie, and some of the others from the Hub, and then I saw Ben run up to me. He looked sad but was pleased to see me. Poor guy. I don't think he really understood.

'Ellis!' he said.

'Hiya, Ben. What are you up to these days?'

'Work,' he said proudly.

'What kind of work?'

'I am a litter picker.'

'So, you're a womble?' I teased.

'Don't be silly.'

'Do you enjoy it?'

'I do. I go and clean up the muck that everyone leaves behind. I am helping out the community.'

'That's good,' I said. 'Though if some people weren't so disgusting there wouldn't be any need. And if the people who were in charge of how we supplied and sold food and gadgets thought of better ways to seal the goods they sold, that would decrease the rubbish as well.'

'I guess so,' said Ben, looking down at the floor.

I felt bad for what I said, especially given the circumstances. I rested my hand on Ben's shoulder. 'So, thank God there are people like you then, eh? You make this community of ours proud. I hope they're paying you for it, though.'

'No, I am a volunteer. Like you and Nathan.'

I heard his voice change at the mention of Nathan's name. We were standing in the corner of the pub. I could see his mother sitting at a table talking to Lottie.

'Nathan would be proud of you,' I said.

Ben looked at me and smiled. 'You think so?'

'I know so.'

'How?'

'Because even though we can't see him, I can hear him. And so can you.'

'I can?'

'Yes. Whenever you think in your head, and you try to decide what the right thing to do is, and you have another thought talking to you, that's Nathan.'

'But I had those thoughts before Nathan went away.'

'Yes, it's called your conscience, but when someone close to you goes away, they become a part of you. So, in the future, he'll be the one guiding you in the right direction.'

'Nathan will help me?'

I nodded. 'He'll support you, just like he always did, but you'll make the final decisions. You're independent. You're an individual. I am proud of you, Ben.'

Ben smiled. 'I got a girlfriend.'

I laughed affectionately. 'Brilliant. What's her name?'

'Adele.'

'The singer?'

'Don't be silly, Ellis.' He pointed over to the bar, where a young woman was chatting to Taz. Then I looked back at him.

'I miss Nathan,' he said.

'We all do, Ben, but that's okay, because if we didn't miss him that would be a lot worse.'

'It would?'

'Yes,' I said.

'Why is that?' he asked me.

'Because it would mean that we didn't care about him, but we do. We love him and missing him is our respect.'

'You're a care worker.'

'We all are, Ben. Or at least we all should be.'

'I am – I am your boss.'

'Okay, you're my boss, but on one condition.'

'What's that, Ellis?'

'I don't think I can be funny man anymore, so I want you to be.'

'But I like you being funny man – you make me laugh.'

'But I can't be when Nathan isn't here.'

'He is. Nathan is up in the sky, and the sky is a lovely place. It's where all the nice people go when they fall asleep and can't wake up anymore.'

I smiled but could feel my eyes filling up with tears. 'It's a nice thought,' I said to him.

'Please don't stop being funny, Ellis; we need someone like you to make us forget the sadness.'

'You're funny yourself, Ben. You make us laugh, so why don't you focus on that?'

'Because Nathan liked you because you were funny, so don't change who you are. That's what would upset Nathan the most. Before you came to the Hub, Nathan was nice and helped us, but he was grumpy. You made him fun, and that's why you shouldn't change.'

I was taken aback at what Ben had said. One, because I'd never heard him talk so deeply before, and secondly, because I never knew. But it all made sense now. The reason the Hub was so happy that I was there was not just because of all the work, ideas and fun I brought there, because Nathan did that already. It was because I was the only one that made Nathan happy.

'Thank you, Ben,' I said. 'What you just said to me is the most important thing I have ever heard. I won't forget it.'

He went in and hugged me and said, 'You will be okay, funny man.'

I went outside and stood in the shelter looking out at the rain. Lottie came out and stood next to me. 'You okay, Ellis?' she said.

I nodded.

'Will you promise me something?' she said.

I looked at her but didn't say a word.

'Please promise me you will never blame yourself for this. You're a lovely boy, Ellis, and Nathan knew that too. You helped him a lot.'

'It's why you all loved me, isn't it?'

She looked at me with confusion.

'You loved me because I brought Nathan back. I brightened him up, and that helped him brighten up the Hub. Isn't that true?'

'To an extent,' she said. 'But not all of it. Everyone loved you because of who you are, Ellis, and everyone loved Nathan for who he was. But what everyone loved the most was Ellis and Nathan being happy together. When you were together it was as if you made everyone happy. You two were special, but when you were together, you made everyone else feel special.'

There was a pause and then I said, 'You lost one of your sons today.'

She nodded and wiped her eyes. 'Yes, but that lady there,' she said while she pointed over to Moira, who was sat talking to a group of relatives, 'she lost her real son.'

'We were your real sons as well; we were if that's what you want. And I'll always be in touch,' I said.

'Thank you, Ellis, I appreciate that.'

There was a silence again and then Lottie said, 'I have one more thing to say.'

'What's that?' I said, trying to hold it together. I could see she was doing the same.

'You two were the most caring people, because you volunteered to do that job. You weren't paid; you did it from the goodness of your hearts.'

'No, that's not true. We're not angels, Lottie. I did it because I had to gain experience. Nathan did it for the same reasons, but initially he was there just because he was unwell himself.'

'Yes, but he got better, and you gained enough

experience, but you both kept coming back. I don't think you would have kept at it in other jobs. You made so many friends at the Hub, and you enjoyed it because you care, and that's why all the service users cared for Nathan and you. They knew you came to care. It wasn't a job, it was a life choice, a human choice, and this is why I know you will come back, eventually.'

'Sorry, Lottie, I won't be coming back.'

'Give it time, you will, I know you will.'

'I miss him, Lottie. I miss Nathan so much. It's only been three weeks, and I can't bear it. I want him back.'

Then I cried and Lottie threw her arms around me and squeezed me tight. 'It's okay, we all miss him, we always will, but we must carry on. He would want that.'

I didn't respond. I just continued to cry.

REMISSION

Today was a good day; in fact, it was the best day of my life. We were informed at the hospital that Jessica's cancer was in remission. She was always a fighter. She did it: she's on the mend. Of course she's still lost and damaged. But her parents and I were over the moon. Even Jessica's mother ran up to me and gave me a huge hug. Did this mean I was forgiven?

I rang and told my parents the good news, and they were crying down the other end of the phone. 'Oh, Ellis, this is wonderful,' said Mam. 'Send her our love.'

Of course, my mam works there, so occasionally we bump into her when we come for Jessica's appointments. But she's been off recently, as she's been making the most of her lieu time.

This was a joyous day. I didn't go out with Zoe that time she got back from her business trip, but we decided that we will go out in the next couple of days and spend a lovely day with Jessica. Just the three of us.

FUNNY MAN

Two weeks after the funeral I came into the Hub. I had arranged to meet Kim. I hadn't even started the job yet and I was already handing in my resignation.

Kim took me into the room where I'd had my induction. I couldn't believe that this place that had always brought me a warm and happy atmosphere, full of bright colours, was now bringing me the complete opposite.

Kim doubled-checked with me that I was sure I didn't want to still come there. I told her I just couldn't. I didn't tell Kim this, but the reason I couldn't ever work there again was because that was the reason why Nathan died in the first place. I had got a full-paid job, and he hadn't. That's how it all started to go downhill.

I gave Kim a hug, thanked her for all her support and then I left.

I walked home, thinking about Nathan. I almost felt like I was going to break down and cry, but I held it together.

The happy time at the Hub, I couldn't do it anymore. I know Ben told me to be funny, but funny is not the same as happy. I would continue to be funny without even realising, I guess, because that's what happened most of the time when I was with Nathan. I guess that's who I am. Funny man.

But I just couldn't go back at the Hub and work there, I just couldn't. They would all forget about me eventually, and they would all be fine. I knew they would. Didn't mean I wouldn't miss them all to bits (well, most of them), but anyway, I would see them about the place, and they wouldn't miss me as much as I missed Nathan.

NATURE

I walk along the grass and contemplate. I ignore the busy traffic ahead and instead I absorb the sweet sounds of Mother Nature. The air, the rustle of leaves and a song from a bird. The jeremiads of the tired earth underneath my feet as I unsettle it from its sleep. I can hear it, because my body almost feels like a ghost waiting to be pulled below the terrain and my soul split into a thousand pieces into the seeds of this world.

The sun is dazzling the sky like treasure and keeping the flowers and grass below pristine. I gently stroke every tree I pass and whisper gratitude, because without them I wouldn't live. No life of mine can be cherished without these natural ICUs.

I appreciate nature because it's the only thing that keeps me going. I don't want to live life the way others do, but that doesn't mean I want to die. It just means I want to live life how it should be, which is just being. Death makes you realise that life is sacred. When I experienced grief for the first time it helped me put everything into perspective. Life is a wonderful thing, but it goes so quickly, and sometimes it will go even quicker than that. Zoe says that there's going to be a lot more death soon. She's heard that there's some kind of pandemic coming, but I haven't paid much attention.

I walk endlessly to try and understand why we are here and what our purpose is. I do this because I find it difficult to know. My hopes, my dreams and desires. They all seem far away, blocked off like a barricade.

The truth is I was born, but not because the world wanted me, so what I want out of the world doesn't matter. But I'm coming to terms with that. Maybe I'm just here to help others. Just because I wasn't expected, doesn't mean people don't want me here.

I've had a small epiphany recently. The people I love, I have not been engaging with them. My mam, dad, Nana, my friends – even Aunty Mel. If I start to make more of an effort to be myself again, the Ellis that everyone used to know, then perhaps they will feel happier, because I am happier, knowing that the world is about being with the ones you love. It's all well and good to have the backdrop of nature, but it can only truly be nurtured if you nurture the people in it.

Perhaps Jessica would be more like herself if I made the effort to be more like myself. I pick her up whenever I can, and I support her, but I don't act like me. I am always appearing sad. Next time I see her, I will tell her jokes, I will laugh and I will be making stupid observations. Because that's what's needed from me. The people that I love, they need that from me, and so I should give it to them. It will make them pleased. They will feel happy and hopefully that will make me feel happy as well.

I must go and visit my parents today, and Nana, and be the old Ellis, because they must feel like they have lost me, like I feel I have lost Jessica. But I am still here, and so is she. So, if I spend some time with them, and be my old self, then that should be a good start to recovery.

Then I will take Jessica out and I will treat her to a lovely day out with the Ellis she used to know, and not this strange old carer she's been dealing with these last few years. After that, I will make Zoe a meal and that will make her feel good. And maybe next week, I'll pop into the Hub and see how everyone's doing. I can do it. I must move on.

There will come a time when I lose everybody, so I must make the most of my time with them now. The person I lost and love will meet me again in the stars, and so will everyone else that I love, when their time comes. Our bodies dissolve, but our love for one another stays forever. Perhaps it's that that operates the trees.

Goodbye for now, Nathan. I will always love you. See you in the sky. Don't wait for me. I will be there with you when my time comes. For now, just keep skateboarding on that halfpipe, because that's what heaven is: it's what you most desire. So when I die, I know you will be there to take my hand.

But for now, I will carry on, and I will continue to listen to the people that need me. The ones with the vulnerable voices.

Some people say they have a slice of life; well, I think I've had the whole meal.

BOOK CLUB QUESTIONS

1. The story contains a lot of references to contemporary politics and culture. In what years do you think it's set?
2. Why do you think the book is set in Yorkshire? How would it be different if it were set somewhere else?
3. Why did Jessica break up with Ellis? Do you think she ever regretted this?
4. What do Ellis and Nathan's musical choices say about them as characters?
5. How does the way Ellis sees the Hub's service users differ from how others see them?
6. Was Kim right or wrong to offer Ellis the job over Nathan? Was Nathan's reaction unreasonable, or did he have a point?
7. How does Ellis' relationship with his parents, Barry and Sandra, compare with other characters' relationships with their parents?
8. Which characters are the 'vulnerable voices' of the title? Are there any characters you think are NOT vulnerable?
9. How reliable is Ellis as a narrator? Do you believe everything he tells you?
10. What will happen next in Ellis' life?

ACKNOWLEDGMENTS

I would like to say a big thank you to my partner George, and to my mum and dad.

Alysia Mayo, Angie Johnson, Denise Quarrington, Stephen Jones, Sarah Griffiths, Kate Westlake, Andrew Price and all the other people I worked with and supported over the years who became good friends.

To all the punk rock bands that I listened to back then that had a big impact on me. (Strange how now I listen mostly to classical music).

I mentioned a lot of the punk bands in the book but I didn't manage to fit in one called Army of Freshmen, so let me just say here, thank you for your amazing music!

The Book Guild for believing in this story and thank you to anyone who has read or seen any of my stories and enjoyed them.

For writing and publishing news, or recommendations of new titles to read, sign up to the Book Guild newsletter: